Charles & Cathy

I hope you enjoy this
literary journey.

Peace & Love

[signature]

An erotic thriller by

ADRIENE ALLEN

PUBLISHED BY ADRIENE ALLEN
11585 Jones Bridge Road, Suite 420
Alpharetta, Georgia 30022

Cover Illustration and layout: St. Jones®
Text layout: Jonathan Gullery

Cataloging-in-Publication Data is on file with the Library of Congress.

ISBN 978-0-615-19059-4

PRINTED IN THE UNITED STATES OF AMERICA

First Edition, November 2007

Lovingly Dedicated to my Husband

Brinson Allen

Our journey together has been one of absolute amazement…
there will never be enough words to express
what it has meant to me, exploring life with you.

I celebrate you, our love & our shared spiritual awakening…

In Memory of
John Henry Williams
Rilla Williams
Percell Erquhart, Sr.
Percell Erquhart, Jr.
Walter Taylor

Acknowledgments

As many of you know, I'm a brand new author, eagerly committed to successfully establishing myself within the literary community. For as long as I can remember I have loved the art of writing. With maturity has come the discovery that writing is truly my passion and God seems to have blessed me with whatever talent readers will perceive. The unveiling of this revelation was no accident. A series of revelatory experiences contributed to my new outlook on life.

Those life lessons taught me that there is a positive growth opportunity with each trial that life presents. While I would love to take all the credit for pulling my outlook together, I cannot. There are many to thank.

First and foremost I must thank God for blessing me considerably. I am also grateful to my entire family; you are all so very important to me. My parents, John and JoeAnn, are phenomenal nurturers, leaders, and two of my best friends. Dad, thank you for allowing me to be a spoiled brat even at the age thirty-nine. Furthermore, Dad, without all your love, lectures and the time spent with me I would not have had the courage to enter this hyper-competitive business world and utilize my entrepreneurial acumen. Mommy, you are so smart; all women can learn something from you. I certainly have. You are a true matriarch and the power source that keeps our family moving in a progressive direction. Your love, support and understanding has empowered me in so many ways, including writing this novel. But a Grandmother's love and encouragement can't be beaten, hands down. I am so fortunate to still have you, Grandma, to hold, to learn from and to laugh with. Even your flirtatious competition for my

7

husband's affections is endearing - he is smitten with you and I am happy to share him with you. Our entire family appreciates your contributions toward making us all better people.

Ari, my princess…you've grown up and blossomed into a beautiful, mature and outgoing young lady. We are so very proud of you and thank you for being my number one fan. You have contributed mightily to this novel. J.O. and Regina, thank you for giving me two precious nephews, Alex and Braxton. I look forward to watching them become perfect gentlemen.

Many people less fortunate than me are forced to 'cope' or 'deal' with their in-laws. I can truly say that my husband's family has been nothing but good to me. My mother in-law, Marcia, is the sweetest. How rare is that? And even more rare is a sister in-law like Angela, a terrific mother to Vincent and Destiny, who loves her brother so much that I get the left over love and still that's plenty! Without Steve and Angela, this book wouldn't have been possible, so thank you for your love and support. I can't forget my Pop; you're the coolest father in-law ever.

The older I've gotten, the more the term friendship has changed in definition as well as its significance. Hoping that no one will feel over looked or offended (because all of my friends are dear to me and contribute to my life in so many wonderful ways), I've selected a few very dear friends to personally acknowledge. I want to give a "high five" and lots of love to my three childhood girlfriends: Cassandra Miller, Elsie Coleman and Aretha Hudson. I'm blessed to have 'home girls' that after thirty-something years, I can still say my heart is always with you, I'm blessed to know you and I'll always love you. As Justin Timberlake has said in song, "we're bringing sexy back…" To my best friend and talented interior designer Tamie Mitchell, please know that I've appreciated each and every year of our long friendship. Thank you for the trillions of hours of girl talk, hanging on the phone while watching TV shows, keeping me up with the latest fashions, traveling, hanging out with our kids, sharing our dramas, and laughing at ourselves while daring anyone else to. I'm convinced the daily doses of keeping things real are what're keeping us young! On a more serious note, you're the sister I've never had and I couldn't possibly love you more if we were.

Recently I acquired special new friends and I address them as "my sisters in greatness"… Dorothea Gates, Charlotte Lusby and Evelyn Mims, you ladies inspire me - all in different ways. Dorothea, remember you told me that I would be writing these books. I fought hard and here I am! You were right about this and so much more.

While the credits may appear that somehow I'm a one woman show, let me make something clear: I was privileged to have the valuable support of many people in making this dream a reality:

St. Jones® you are a visionary and thanks to you I have two spectacular websites: www.adrieneallen.com and www.atrocitywithin.com. I have found the editorial and consulting services of Pat Barnhart's Writing Down Pat of tremendous value throughout the completion of this project.

Brinson, honey, thank you for believing in me…you single handedly inspired me to go for it, putting all else aside. I am grateful for your allowing me to explore and take all the time I've needed to make this book a reality. You're a Godsend and you mean the world to me.

To conclude this way may seem strange, but I'd like to give advance appreciation and thanks to those who read *Atrocity Within* and adopt it into your literary lives… this includes the highly experienced literary agency with lots of clout that I'm sure is out there; a publisher that will welcome my ambition, and will partner with me to achieve critical acclaim and commercial success and introduce me to the worldwide market place; and of course, an editor that will take my words and raise them to new heights.

Last but certainly not least, I'd like to thank you, the reader, for supporting me in this journey and giving my literary material a chance to be known. I am hopeful that you will find my work worthy of your devotion; in return I will do my literary best to keep you fulfilled and pleasantly entertained.

Adriene Allen
Atlanta, Georgia
October 2007

-Chapter 1-

A night not forgotten

It was meant to be a night to remember, and no one there would have ever forgotten it. One of those glittering milestones that get talked about from one generation to another. The charismatic Attorney General of the United States was scheduled to attend; the Secret Service had swept the building repeatedly and declared it secure.

As Elle Corday-Whitmire fastened the clasp on her triple strand of rare Tahitian black pearls, she decided that she deserved this night. She had fought like hell to get where she was and tonight her grand achievement was to be acknowledged. So what if there were backs with gouges in them from her Jimmy Choos. So what if a few hearts had been not just broken, but smashed like cardiac road kill. This night was worth it all.

What she saw in the mirror was, in her humble opinion, pure exotic perfection. Why not be honest? After all, she'd been told by both men and women that she was as juicy and delicious as a ripe Asian pear, and she'd worked hard at that too. The necklace was her most recent trophy; a gift from her husband that morning over breakfast. He had dropped them into a glass of champagne, 'to start the day off right', he said.

A nagging worry drew her almond shaped eyes down to her dressing table, where four rough cut pieces of brilliant jade sat, lined up like little tear drops on the glass surface. The anonymous notes that had accompanied three of them, one by one, were tucked securely in the back of her lingerie drawer.

"Fuck you," she said, returning to her reflection. "You're not going to ruin this night, no matter who sent you."

She smoothed a few imaginary wrinkles from the sleek Valentino original, his version of the little black dress hand sewn in a size 4 just for her. There was a slight similarity to the one he'd designed for Julia Roberts, but only the neckline. It revealed just enough cleavage to attract attention, but not so much that it looked 'tacky' as the women of Atlanta liked to say. It also showed just enough of her long, shapely legs so that men's minds would travel up them to their nexus, that Holy Land of lush Asian-American strangeness that had been her calling card when her name had been Jade.

Access to that 'Holey Land' of plenty pussy was now supposedly the exclusive purview of her husband, Harrison T. Whitmire III, Georgia's senior Senator, and he was eternally grateful. He loved her, he spoiled her, and he would die or kill for her. At least she hoped he would, if it ever came to that.

Walking out of his masculine, leather appointed dressing room wearing only black socks and a Rolex watch, he interrupted her thoughts.

"Elle, honey, you look spectacular. The old men in your firm are going to have erections so big they'll fall over on their faces at the martini bar and embarrass themselves. The Secret Service agents will think they're hiding concealed weapons."

"Harrison, how you do exaggerate," she replied. "Good thing you're a politician and given naturally to hyperbole and verbosity, or I might think you were just full of crap."

"Aw, Darlin', your vocabulary is exceeded only by your beauty. Being just a humble Georgia boy and a servant of the people, I never quite know if you're insulting me or paying me a compliment. Now come here. Daddy needs a quickie before we face all those sour old lawyers dying to fuck my wife."

The High Museum of Art had been selected for the reception honoring the ascension to full partner by Elle Corday-Whitmire. Office manager

Clarice Povitch had been given the task of arranging the affair, and even though she had mixed feelings about the honoree, she was dedicated to the firm's senior partner, loved him in fact, and chose the site with great care. Her goal was to select a venue that reflected well on the firm's image, was easily accessible in a city where access was nearly an impossibility, and would be deemed suitable by government security.

The High was currently presenting *Louvre Atlanta,* in partnership with the prestigious Musée du Louvre in Paris, which included hundreds of master pieces from the Louvre's collections. In order to hold their special reception, Clarice had secured exclusive access to the Wieland Pavilion Grand Lobby and two gallery levels, with first class catering included.

Her reward for this coup was the privilege of getting down on her knees under her boss's desk and giving him a lengthy and satisfying blow job. She was honored. After all, he could have chosen most anyone to do it- the assistants, researchers, interns or law clerks would have been more than willing to 'do' the old man. He was known for his generous promotions to those whom he deemed team players. She suspected the evening's honoree had been on her knees a few times under that big desk, but couldn't prove it in a court of law.

The museum, a Richard Meier design that is the centerpiece of the Woodruff Arts Center complex, not only houses works of art, but the building itself is considered by many to be a work of art in its own right. The building is a dazzling white - porcelain tiles comprise the exterior - with an equally pristine white interior anchored by a sun-drenched, four-story atrium.

Clarice also chose the museum because she felt the proximity to art would provide a more cultured ambiance for the affair than the typical hotel meeting room or restaurant. She hoped that if the event was a success, Elle would appreciate it and she would get credit and recognition for a job well done. Even though she despised the new partner for perceived slights in the past, and loved Ernest Carlyle dearly, she was also attracted to Elle on a deeply instinctual level. She sensed strong sexual undercurrents barely hidden by a thin veneer of professionalism. She wouldn't mind one bit getting on her knees under Elle's desk. She was indeed one hell of a lawyer, but first and foremost, she was a woman in every sense of the word. That, Clarice had known from their first encounter the day Elle arrived at the firm as a mere attorney, hired because they needed to fill their quota for minorities. Elle had accounted for two: Asian and female.

This was an important night for the firm and they fully expected a lot of press coverage. Any time The Whitmires were involved, there was sure to be a photographer snapping their pictures, as they were a made for publicity couple. Not to mention the Attorney General had accepted an invitation and therefore publicity was ensured.

More than the wife of a senator, or a mere rainmaker, Elle had caused thundering torrential downpours of money to flow into the coffers of Carlyle, Kilpatrick, Powell and Whitmire, LLP.

Her successful handling of a recent merger - Southern Bell Company had engineered the hostile takeover of a huge Chinese wireless telecommunications company - had made her partnership inevitable, even though old man Carlyle was not completely on board. Something about her didn't seem right to him, although he certainly wouldn't turn down a roll in the hay with her. He had seventy million dollars stashed in a Cayman bank, though, and really didn't give a damn anymore. Let the younger ones worry about whatever shit she would 'rain' down on their heads. He would play their little politically correct game and welcome the mixed-breed cunt to the firm. Next thing you knew, they'd be hiring some damned Yankee Negro to join the firm. When they did that, he'd just sail off on his 90-foot Hatteras and to hell with them. Maybe take old Clarice with him. She was no looker but she sure gave good head.

The fifty or so guests, all elegantly dressed, gathered in the High's hushed and rarified atmosphere, sipping peach martinis and nibbling at sushi, Beluga caviar crepes, and other exotic delicacies. Many of them wished the caterer had served miniature country ham biscuits or tiny cornbread canapés, but pretended to enjoy the haute cuisine. A photographer from

Atlanta Journal-Constitution moved among the guests snapping pictures; he was killing time waiting for the arrival of the guest of honor. He had also learned from his sources that the U.S. Attorney General, Raoul Salazar, would attend. CNN had sent a videograpgher and a reporter who stood on the lower curved ramp, positioned to capture the arrival of Elle and Harrison Whitmire, Atlanta's version of Camelot.

One legal secretary commented to another as they stood pretending to admire the Claes Oldenburg and Coosie van Bruggen sculpture titled *Balza/Pentaque*, "Good grief, such a big fuss for that woman. This must be costin' a fortune. They coulda given us all a raise and the money woulda been better spent. She's just another damn lawyer, right?"

"Oh, calm down, Miranda," said her co-worker. "You know they did it up big when Charlie Powell made partner. They can't exactly do less for the first woman partner. You're just jealous 'cause she has bigger boobs than yours and she didn't have to buy them. I think she's hotter than a 4th of July barbecue. Hell, I'm not gay but I'd do her in a heart beat."

Miranda rolled her eyes, but secretly agreed. Even though Elle often treated her poorly, requesting revision after revision to pleadings, calling her incompetent and threatening to fire her, she had to admit the woman oozed sex. She smelled like sex and exploited her feminism at every possible turn.

Conversation stopped and everyone turned toward the sleek bank of elevators as they heard the doors whoosh open. Elle stepped out on the arm of her tall, gray haired husband, adjusting strands of lustrous ebony pearls with her free hand.

They were immediately surrounded by well-wishers and fawning firm employees, the CNN reporter diligently capturing it all on camera.

"Miz Whitmire," said the reporter, pushing a microphone toward Elle's face, "how does it feel to be the first woman partner of a firm that's been an all male Atlanta institution for nearly a hundred years?"

Elle smiled, tilting her head toward the camera. "It feels wonderful, of course, I just hope that I can live up to everyone's expectations and continue to contribute to the success of the firm. At Carlyle, Kilpatrick,

Powell and now Whitmire, which I must admit sounds wonderful to say out loud, it is truly a team effort. I'm just one member of a remarkable team."

Nicely said, but bullshit, thought the reporter. *You better earn your keep every day or these fuckers will dump you like a fat, ugly blind date.*

As soon as the Whitmire's elevator doors closed, an adjacent elevator's door slid open and two men in off the rack JC Penney suits stepped out, scanning the room, their hands folded behind them. Their clean shaven faces, short haircuts, and serious demeanor instantly identified them as law enforcement.

Just as the reporter was about to ask another question, they approached Elle and Harrison, stepping in front of the reporter and cameraman, blocking their access to the power couple.

"Elle Corday-Whitmire?" asked the taller of the two men.

"Why, yes," she responded, a bit confused by the presence of these obvious party crashers, even though one of them looked vaguely familiar. She could swear she'd seen him naked in a hot tub and could envision a very hairy chest beneath the cheap white shirt.

He pulled a leather folder from his pocket, flashed a badge, and said more loudly than necessary, "F.B.I., ma'am. I am agent Warner and this is my partner, agent Tomlinson. You are under arrest. Please come with us."

He quickly took her by the arm, turned her around, and agent Tomlinson snapped a pair of plastic handcuffs on her that he had pulled from his belt.

The partners, wives and associates of the firm could only stare as their star, their rain maker, their newest full partner, was led roughly away. It was all caught on tape by CNN - Elle's outraged expression and Harrison's face gone white with shock - but the newspaper reporter, who had been politely waiting her turn, was left with an empty notebook. She knew she was screwed. If this was turning from a social event to a crime story, another reporter would be assigned. She snapped open her cell phone and called the assignment editor to find out what she should do.

Ernest Carlyle ate the olive out of his freshly shaken dry martini, and couldn't have been any happier or smiled any bigger if he had been at David Duke's presidential inauguration. This had turned out to be a really un-fucking-believable night.

Chapter 2

Meeting Roxy

To understand the shocking events I'm going to tell y'all about, you need to understand my city: Atlanta. Actually, Atlanta is not so much a city, as it is a spider web of little connected communities - some quite bright and shiny, and some very dark and sticky.

The very reason Atlanta exists at all is because it's a crossroads; there's even a joke about dying - before you get to heaven or hell, you gotta go through Atlanta.

There's a big ole ring road around Atlanta - we call it 'the loop', and you're either inside the loop or you're outside. I like to think of it as a metaphorical 'loop'. Sort of like a noose some say, or being in the know or out to lunch.

The Atlanta Braves baseball team had a new player once who missed his first game because he got stuck on the loop, just going round and round Atlanta and couldn't figure out how to get off!

Congestion and urban sprawl have caused lots of beautiful little towns and communities to get sucked in to the huge spider web. Charming places like Alpharetta, Sandy Springs, Decatur, Marietta and Hapeville have become part of the larger 'greater Atlanta'. Although some have managed to hang onto their individuality, they all reflect a newer, broader diversity and an openness to, um, alternate lifestyles more so than their forefathers might have exactly foreseen.

My point is, I guess, don't think of Atlanta as a l'il ole Southern city, because you'd be mistaken. Atlanta is in the South, but Honey, it's about as Southern as Broadway and as small town as Copenhagen, Paris, or Harlem. Diversity is not just a talkin' point here, it's a description. Everything and anything goes. Competing lifestyles coexist in relative peace, from the white glove prim and proper whites only Country Clubs (yes, they do still exist), to entire gay and transsexual communities, we got it all. The bodacious black women in their huge Sunday go to meetin' hats live in harmony (and sometimes armed conflict) with the gangs, yuppies, gays, illegal Mexicans, well dressed business executives, silver tongued politicians, super wealthy, ten dollar street hookers, and thousand dollar call girls.

It's mostly the dark and sticky side of Atlanta's web I deal with in my business, but the messy stuff pays for a lot of the bright and shiny, so it's a trade off I'm quite willin' to make. Turns out some folks don't agree, but before I get ahead of myself and get my wagon in front of my pony, let's go back to the start. Back when things were about to get very sticky indeed.

My name is Roxy by the way - Roxanne Porter to be honest about it - and both men and women find me attractive. I decided a long time ago that my looks were my best asset, so I've had a few things enhanced, but that's all you need to know. I also have some interesting tattoos and gold rings, and for the right price you can see those. Maybe even taste or touch.

Folks tend to under estimate me, the dumb blonde Southern belle stereotype, and that's okay. When I get my highly polished nails into 'em, they never see me coming.

My business, *Hot'lanta Belles,* has grown from just me and a few amateur working girls servicing johns in cheap motels and learning how to provide upscale escort services, to being a very exclusive brothel housed in a luxurious mansion in none other than the snooty environs of Buckhead. I also have expanded my business over the last few years to three other cities - Las Vegas, Nashville, and Chicago - each place under a different name. Seems like the more women want to 'have it all' with careers, kids and marriage too, the marriage gets the short end of the stick so to speak.

They are too damn tired to take care of their men, but my girls are never too tired. They make a man feel like a million bucks so he can go home to his 'super wife' more relaxed and ready to take care of the 'honey do' list and play with the kiddies. Guess you could say I'm in the *piece* keeping business, sorta like the United Nations of Sex.

It raised a few eyebrows in the real estate closing when I opened a Prada handbag and tossed stacks of cash on the table, but don't think for a minute the realtors, lawyers, or any of the property owners were going to turn up their noses. They jumped on that money like pussy cats on cream and I was suddenly the owner of an Italianate three-story estate on four gentrified acres of prime real estate located on West Paces Ferry, in the heart of Buckhead. There are formal gardens and statuary as well as state-of-the-art electronics and toys. The places in the other cities are unique to the areas, but they are all lavish mansions with walls, gates and heavy security.

Here in Buckhead I spent more money turning the ten bedrooms into private suites, each with its own bathroom and Jacuzzi, built in wide-screen television, and armoires filled with some of those toys and batteries. Come one, come all, I always say! After an unfortunate set-to one New Year's Eve when two of my clients got into a shooting match, the news media dubbed me the Buckhead Madam, a title I am quite proud of. With what I paid out in money under the table, I wasn't worried about being closed down. In fact, the publicity was great for business. Besides, as any person who deals in the sex business will tell you, mixing sexual tension, emotions, guilt, jealousy and other pressures that my clients have to deal with, you are bound to get an explosion sooner or later.

Anyway, staffing my business was a challenge right from the start. You gotta have a nice variety of ladies so the clients have a choice. I also like my girls to be smart so they can talk to the clients about more than soap operas or what's on sale at K-Mart. Unlike street girls and the ones who work the 'out call' side of the business, my girls get regular medical checkups too.

I wanted to establish a good clientele - business men, politicians, rich college brats - and they like to pretend they're having a 'relationship' not just getting their ashes hauled. That means conversation. It also requires some play acting ability on the part of my girls. They have to make the client feel like they're important, that the girl cares about them and wants to make them happy. Hell, if they could get that at home, they wouldn't be paying my prices.

One of the first girls I hired was a beautiful black girl named Lashonda Johnson, but she went professionally by the name Noir. She was stunning - tall and slender but lots of curves. If you looked up 'bootylicious' in the dictionary, her picture would be there. Of course, I auditioned her myself. I'm pretty hard to please - been around the block a few times you might say - and she had me begging for mercy. That girl's tongue had a muscular life of its own - pure strong yet soft magic. Even after I hired her, and even though I have a great steady boyfriend, anytime I really needed a good orgasm, I went to Noir. So many men leave a woman 'unfinished'; they're just concerned about their own 'coming and going' so to speak, that even us professionals need a good servicing now and again.

She became popular with both men and women clients and often had a waiting list for appointments. Noir had another very useful talent - she could be as street and ghetto as a client might wish, or she could be uptown sophisticated. I've even heard her adopt a pretty good French accent, as though she might be Polynesian. Listen, the girl might be black, but she is a true chameleon and a damn good actress.

Another one of my stars was a college student who called herself Jade, but her real name was Elle Corday. Part American and part Korean, Elle had that kind of exotic beauty that men crave. She was tall and slender but with nice, round boobs and a full power muff with long silky, luxuriant hair that you could lose your fucking mind over. Most girls now like to shave completely or leave a neat little triangle, but not Jade. And her eyes just pulled you into her aura like magnets. They were dark chocolate brown, nearly black, with flecks of gold, long lashes and that Asian almond slant that makes you think 'smart and wise'.

Jade worked for me all through her college years and while she went to law school, and she made a ton of money. She even helped me with my never ending bookkeeping chores - keeping two sets of books is always a challenge -and she had a head for math and a devious mind that made her a real asset.

Her family was dirt poor, and even though she earned a scholarship, she still needed lots of money for law school, books, and jewelry. The girl loved jewelry and her clients often rewarded her with trinkets, especially pieces of jade. She once told me she was sorry she hadn't named herself Emerald or Diamond because those stones were more valuable than jade.

The man who introduced her to me and suggested that I hire her had been her client when she worked at an out-call agency in Athens, Georgia and he advised her to come and see me. It was safer, smarter and better money he told her, to work for an in-call outfit. He continued to avail himself of her services, but letting them remain so chummy would turn out to be a mistake in judgment on my part, but that story will come later.

Chapter 3

The Transformation of Ellie

llie Corday grew up in Pulaski, Virginia, an impoverished and humble coal mining town with only one saving grace - a beautiful winding river - unless you count the gray stone courthouse that has a deceptive look of solid justice to it. In reality, the poor coal miners and their families rarely got any justice in Pulaski.

She was born Ellie Eun Mi Corday to parents of American and Korean heritage. Thomas Corday had enlisted in the Army the day he turned eighteen, hoping to become an engineer and make more money than his father had as a grocer. Instead, the Army stuck him in a vehicle maintenance corps and shipped him to Korea. He was a simple small town boy, a virgin, and an idealist and fell head over heels in love with the first Korean girl he fucked. Her name was Joo-Eun Mi and she gave him his first orgasm not produced by his own calloused hand.

Love at first sight might be too strong, but they did quickly fall in love (she was only too willing to 'love you long time' to get a shot at the American dream), married when she got pregnant, and he sent her home to Pulaski to live with his parents until his tour of duty was over. Their first born, a son, conceived in Korea but born in the United States, was spoiled by his grandparents and adored by his lonely and isolated mother.

Foreign wars always produce lots of mixed marriages and in turn, thousands of mongrel children, but it is rare to find a pleasing combination of features, as anyone knows who ever played Mr. Potato Head. Thomas Junior, with an oddly configured body and face, was visual proof.

In November of 1953 Thomas came home to a virtual stranger of a wife and a crawling infant son, but was happy to be out of the military. His dreams of becoming an engineer had long since been replaced by the reality of incomprehensible military decisions. He had learned how to paint Jeeps and count munitions, neither of which translated into employment skills in Pulaski. He was glad when he got work in the coal mine. At least he got a decent pay check, a good meal after work and some steady love making whenever he had the energy.

As a welcome home gift, Thomas's parents had presented the couple with a brand new 1968 Chevrolet Malibu 4-door sedan with white wall tires and a gleaming yellow two-tone paint job. They had come to admire the way Joo-Eun had adapted to the American way of life, especially in small town Pulaski, and they were hopeful that with a son and more children sure to come, the couple would prosper and be happy.

One year after returning from military duty, the Corday's welcomed a baby daughter, whom they named Ellie. The results of Ellie's blended gene pool were spectacular when she became an adult, but as a child her looks were a handicap, especially among the scraggly ragamuffins of Pulaski. She was taller than most (her father was six-two), and had waist length shiny black hair. In typical Korean fashion, her mother roughly chopped crude bangs across her forehead and dressed her in ill-fitting clothes and shoes far too large for her thin gangly legs. As a result, she appeared clumsy and strange, even to the other dirt poor children. She was the Chinaman oddity in a town with a nearly pure Caucasian population.

Ellie and her older brother Tommy, a happy go lucky boy who cheerfully embraced his mixed breeding, grew up with no luxuries. Even the basics were sometimes hard to come by. Thomas went to work before dawn in the coal mines, so they rarely saw him. His paycheck barely covered their meager rent and utilities, leaving Joo-Eun to manage the household and meals on mere pennies. By planting her own garden, keeping a few chickens for the eggs, and occasionally humbly asking for help from Thomas's parents, she managed to keep them all fed and clothed.

While living with his parents, Joo-Eun paid close attention when others were speaking and she picked up the English language quickly, although perhaps out of stubborn reluctance to bend to American ways, she spoke broken English throughout her life. She was quiet, not given to starting conversations, and so people frequently assumed that she could not understand English. That gave her plenty of opportunities to learn family and household secrets, and she held those little tidbits 'in her pocket' as her mother would have said, for a rainy day. Her mother had also taught her that to keep a man she must please him, and that she certainly did. Thomas could not have wished for a more fulfilling companion, or one who was more skilled in the exotic Asian ways of love making.

Joo-Eun knew tricks that could arouse her tired husband even after twelve hour shifts in the dark mines where he wielded a pick ax until his shoulders burned with fatigue. He would sometimes be in the shower and would feel her soapy hands rubbing him and his aches and pains would wash down the drain with the soot as his manhood grew and throbbed to her ministrations.

What Joo-Eun and Thomas didn't know was that little Ellie sometimes hid and watched them. From the age of four until she left home, she studied her parents like a curious scientist, trying to understand what they were doing and why it made her father so happy.

She also watched her mother when she was alone, and saw that she cried over old black and white photos of her homeland. Rather than making Ellie curious about Korea however, it made her dislike 'that place' because it seemed to make her mother sad.

One day when she was just starting first grade she felt like a big girl and decided to ask her mother about the pictures.

"Why do you cry, Mommy?" she asked, peeking out from behind the closet door of their bedroom. "Are the pictures sad?"

Joo-Eun was startled to see her daughter's beautiful face peering from behind the door. "You not be snooping, girl," she replied angrily. Joo-Eun had created her own tightly bound life and she refused to let this naughty child into her private moments. "Besides, pictures are about old country, place you never see, people you not ever know. Go way now."

Shut off from her mother, Ellie lived to make her father happy - to see him smile at her the way he smiled at her usually dour and cold mother. What did Mommy have that she didn't? Why didn't Daddy love her like he loved Mommy? Jealousy grew within Ellie like tomatoes in the warm Virginia sun. She continued her secret watching, and she learned a lot. She learned that in spite of what her grandmother said about the way to a man's heart being through his stomach, there was a better way.

One day her mother left to go to the market and Ellie was home alone when her father came home from work. As usual, he removed his shoes at the front door and headed straight for the shower; Joo-Eun had strict rules before allowing anyone to sit on her furniture. To some, her furniture might appear shabby, but she was proud of her American home and worked hard at keeping it spotlessly clean and well organized.

When eleven year old Ellie heard the water running, she quickly stripped out of her clothes and stepped into the shower with her father. He didn't open his eyes.

"Oh, so you're home, my little oriental flower," he said, feeling small hands curling and twisting his pubic hair. "Ahhhh, that feels so good."

Ellie was quite proud of herself at how her father's thing grew magically in her hand. This was pretty neat, but it was also a little frightening. It was much bigger than she had imagined. She also felt something she had not felt before - a wetness between her legs that was not due to the shower. She touched herself to make sure. What was that? Immediately upon touching herself, she felt as though her body was on fire. There was a powerful itch inside her that screamed to be scratched.

Following purely animal instincts, she stood balanced on the sides of the tub, turned her father to face her, and pushed his soapy engorged penis inside her. As soon as it was in as far as she could possibly push it, she wrapped her arms around his neck and her legs around his hips.

Thomas opened his eyes knowing something was very different, but it was too late to change the course of events. He was torn between being horrified - this was his daughter clinging wildly to him - and being driven by desire to complete the act she had so willfully begun.

He closed his eyes again, hugged her tightly to him, and began pumping with a ferocity that he had never felt before. She, this child of his, felt good. Oh, God, she felt good. She was so tight. He bent and suckled at her small breasts, now protruding and engorged with passion, welcoming his teeth and tongue. He was crazed with lust. He pumped harder and faster until he came with a gushing force of hot liquid that washed down her thin thighs and matted in her sparse pubescent bush.

Ellie wanted more, his muscular arms felt so good encircling her, but he put her gently down, stepped out of the shower, wrapped himself in a towel, and walked out of the bathroom, closing the door behind him.

She stood in the shower, rubbing herself and trying to understand what had just happened, until the water began running cold. She splashed away the tiny blood droplets that had collected on the sides of the tub, figuring that her father's thing had been so big it had injured her. It didn't hurt though; it had felt very good.

When she walked out of the bathroom, fully dressed but with wet hair and red cheeks, her mother was standing in the hallway watching her with an unreadable expression on her face.

"Hi, Mother," Ellie said, not certain what the look meant. "Are you back from shopping?"

"Yes, Daughter, I am. But I think I too late."

She turned and walked away. From that day until her death many years later, she never touched Ellie again. She was not unkind to her, but she showed her no affection. Why would one embrace a rival? She also never left her alone with her husband, Ellie's father, again.

Oh, Ellie tried. She'd had a taste of sex and it was like a new burning hunger inside her. She wanted more. Her brother and the other boys her age were useless with their tiny little things; she wanted a man and the only man she knew was her father.

Sometimes she would walk out of the bathroom naked, pretending not to notice that her brother or her father was nearby. She began never wearing panties and once she took her father's hand underneath the dining table and placed it between her legs. He snatched it away nearly spilling his iced tea, but she noticed that leaving the table he had a difficult time walking.

He began bringing her little trinkets - pieces of chocolate candy or dime store toys and placing them under her pillow. Finding them validated her feelings of power over him.

She managed to seduce him one more time before leaving for private school. Her mother had a doctor's appointment that she couldn't avoid and Ellie took full advantage. She loved the feeling of power her body gave her. She learned that she could control a man with her body and by the age of twelve she was as ripe as a piece of summer fruit.

After taking a course on sex education in school, she learned that sex between adults and children, especially family members, was wrong. It was a horrible sin in the church and she became riddled with guilt. For a while. Then the feeling of power and being able to control strong men with one flash of her crotch with its now fully formed black luxuriant bush, was worth the risk of hell and damnation. She learned that even the pious priest, Father Jonathan, was not immune to her powers. She had innocently lifted her little plaid skirt one day during confession and Father Jonathan had gasped and reached out to touch her. He was actually drooling from the side of his mouth as his pale thin fingers stroked clumsily at her.

She quickly pushed her skirt back down - as usual she wore no underpants having found them inhibiting - and stood up admonishing the foolish priest.

"Why Father, isn't that a sin? Touching little girls? Shame on you." She skipped out of the church, giving one last glimpse of true heaven with a flip of her skirt.

"Bye, Father. See you soon."

She wondered if he would get a wink of sleep that night, and was willing to bet (another sin) he wouldn't.

-Chapter 4-

The Great Escape

With her newly found powers and a voracious appetite for learning, Ellie soon outgrew everything Pulaski had to offer. The boys were boring, she had read everything in the library, her mother couldn't stand her, her father vacillated between wanting to fuck her and ignoring her, and her brother was obviously queer because he wouldn't touch her at all.

She had to get out of there. But how? Leaving took money and she had none.

She spoke to the kindly and bespectacled county guidance counselor, Mr. Warmoth, at school, asking him questions about what jobs paid the most money and trying to figure out a future outside of Pulaski.

"Young ladies seem to prefer marriage and babies to high paying careers, Ellie. But if your heart is set on the working world perhaps you would like to be a teacher or a nurse?"

As he handed her some colorful brochures, he dropped one. Ellie quickly bent to pick it up and he caught a glimpse of her bare buttocks.

"Young lady," he said sternly, "you are apparently not abiding by the school's dress code policy. You must wear proper undergarments at all times and I must insist that in future you obey the rules."

"Yes, sir," she replied meekly, smiling up at the tall thin gentleman. "Shall I come again so that you can check?"

Momentarily caught off guard by her boldness, he recovered quickly and said, "Why, yes. I'm here at this school every Tuesday. You come back in her next Tuesday and I will verify your compliance with the dress code.

I'll also have some more brochures for you. But if you are not properly dressed, you will go straight to the principal's office."

"Thank you, sir, I understand. And if you could, sir, I'd like some information on the very best paying jobs. Can girls be doctors?"

"Of course they can, Ellie. Girls can be anything they want to. It's just not often done. As a matter of fact my cousin lives in Pittsburgh and she is an attorney at law and handles big court cases. She makes a great deal of money. Of course, she is not married and has no children as a result. I sometimes worry about her choices." He rubbed his chin and looked pensively out the window.

"That sounds interesting," Ellie replied, deciding to head straight to the library and learn more about what it meant to be an attorney.

She smiled promisingly at Mr. Warmoth and just for fun she dropped her pencil on the way out of his office and bent to retrieve it, giving him one more glimpse of her small, well rounded butt. She thought that might ensure his diligence in bringing her lots of information about her future.

After learning that medical school involved eight years of college and then an internship, she dismissed it and began reading the books she had checked out of the library. She loved the idea that attorneys not only helped people, they had the power to change things. They could help innocent people fight the injustices of the legal system, but they could also get guilty people off Scott free if they were clever enough. She thought she could be clever, but she also knew that law school would cost money.

Her next visit to the counselor's office proved to be productive. This time when she entered, he locked the door and drew the blinds.

"Okay, Ellie. Lift your skirt. It's time for our uniform check."

She did as she was told, and this time she was wearing pink under panties, only she had taken scissors and cut the crotch out.

Now twelve years old, she was well developed. Mr. Warmoth gasped and averted his eyes, but as she continued to stand, holding her skirt above her waist, unphased by his expression, his eyes were drawn back to her crotch.

"Um, Ellie," he said, stammering and trying to catch his breath, "I think I need to measure your under garments for compliance. Stand still for a moment."

He went to his desk and pulled out a ruler, then came around and kneeled before her. Taking the ruler, he placed it against her crotch, first in one direction and then the other, as she looked down upon his balding head.

She smiled victoriously as he bent farther and kissed her crotch, then stood and said, "Good girl. You seem to be in compliance. From now on, you come in here each week and I will provide you with more information, and we will continue to monitor your uniform. You may go now."

She dropped her skirt and left with a fresh stack of information, smiling and skipping down the hall to her next class.

As she continued to visit his office over the following months, his 'uniform checks' became more and more intense, his kisses became deeper and deeper, and he taught her how to take his penis into her mouth and relieve his pain. He schooled her in the proper use of her tongue and how not to bite.

She was glad to do it; her reward was a glowing letter of recommendation on county board of education letterhead, and a steady supply of insider scholarship information that she doubted other students received. Maybe this was her ticket out of Pulaski. So what if his skinny old fingers poked at her? So what if he licked at her like a lollipop? If she closed her eyes she could pretend it was the cute boy who sat next to her in Algebra.

There was a beautiful private academy in Georgia called Darlington School that struck her fancy immediately when she saw it. The glossy brochure showed a picturesque lake, quaint buildings, and girls riding bicycles on wooded paths. Wow. Words like honor and tradition, 'wisdom above knowledge', and academic excellence were sprinkled throughout the brochure like pretty confetti. Perhaps she could regain a better sense of herself there; figure out who she was and what she truly wanted out of life.

Nothing was going to stand in her way. She felt strong and capable, yet somehow sullied and less than beautiful. She suddenly longed for a solid platform and loved the words 'tradition' and 'excellence' that Darlington School seemed to embody. But how would she get the money?

For weeks she pored over the financial aid catalogs and suddenly found something called the McFarland Foundation located in Birmingham, Alabama. They selected and sponsored one girl each school year with funding for room, tuition and books. *That would be perfect*, she thought, and she immediately wrote to the foundation, enclosing the letter from Mr. Warmoth. She pleaded in her very best English grammar (although her mother had taught her both Korean and Japanese) and florid schoolgirl penmanship, putting forth her case that she was of mixed heritage, poor, and desperately wanted a better education. She added a post script that she wanted to study the law to help poor innocent people, hoping that would give her an edge.

After posting the letter, about which she told her parents nothing because she never thought she would get an answer, she religiously met the mailman on the sidewalk every day. He too had begun looking differently at her lately, and he was always happy to see her sitting on the front steps of her little home waiting for his arrival. It made him feel special. One day she gave him a peek at heaven just to make sure he showed up on time and didn't lose her mail. She had now cut the crotch out of all her under panties, and washed them herself to keep her mother from finding out her newest secret.

After two weeks she had nearly given up, but one blistering hot July day there it was - a crisp white envelope with an embossed return address from the McFarland Foundation. Her hands shook as she took that and the rest of the mail from the grinning mailman and ran into the house.

She ripped into the envelope excitedly and read that they were 'proud to offer her a full scholarship to Darlington School for the coming school year, including room, board, books, and a small stipend for miscellaneous expenses'.

All she had to do was have her parents sign the forms enclosed, and present herself at the foundation's offices in Birmingham not later than August 1st. There she would undergo an orientation, be provided with her school supplies, and then transportation would be arranged to Rome, Georgia where Darlington School was located. They had addressed the letter to Elle Corday, because she had changed the spelling of her name when she applied to the foundation. Ellie seemed far too 'country' to her - she wanted to begin her new life as Elle. She had seen that name in a movie star fan magazine and immediately decided that it suited her much better.

At dinner that night, after her mother had conveniently pleasured her father in the shower (Ellie knew, of course, because she had listened at the door to his gurgled moans), she placed the stack of papers in the center of the table and explained to her surprised parents what they were.

"You want to go where?" her father asked. "You are too young to be going off to another state."

Her mother, however, was quite happy.

"Thomas, she not too young. She big girl now. You know?"

Of course he knew. And he knew what his wife meant by the question. He was caught between his wife and his daughter in a situation where he could not win. He was weak and often at the mercy of his desires. He also knew something his wife didn't yet know - the clinic at the mine company had taken some chest x-rays that revealed lung cancer. They called it 'black lung' and he wasn't sure how much longer he could work, although the disease was still in its infancy. He not only couldn't afford to send Ellie away to school, he could barely afford the little trinkets he bought her because he lived for her smiles and the rare touches she allowed him.

Eighteen year old Tommy spoke up.

"Dad, let her go. This is a good chance for her. What the hell is she going to do here in Pulaski? Sell tickets at the movie theater? You know you and Mom can't afford college for her in a couple of years. What's she gonna do, huh?"

"Tommy right, Thomas," Joo-Eun said. "This good chance."

Good chance get her out of house, she thought.

"Well, all right, if you both think so," Thomas reluctantly agreed. He knew in his heart that sending his beautiful daughter away would be like turning off the sunshine. His life would be plunged into darkness as bleak as the mines he toiled in every day. Joo-Eun met his needs the best she could and he was grateful, but it was little Ellie's beauty and the tantalizing hope of once again pushing himself into her tight warmth that kept him going. His dark heart would now match his blackened diseased lungs, and he hoped that God would take him soon.

He sighed deeply and then he and Joo-Eun added their signatures to the complex legal forms just below Elle's, without even reading them. They did both notice that Ellie had changed the spelling of her name, but neither commented. They had already lost their daughter; what difference did losing the name they had given her at birth matter?

The next morning Elle walked straight to the post office and mailed the forms back to the McFarland Foundation. Then she walked six blocks in the other direction to the Greyhound Bus Station to find out how much a ticket from Pulaski to Birmingham, Alabama would cost. She hoped she could somehow scrape together enough money for the fare and a new outfit to wear on her trip from the hopeless poverty of Pulaski to the beautiful green and wooded acres of Darlington School.

Chapter 5

The Education of Elle Begins

To raise money for Elle's trip to Alabama, the Corday family pooled every cent they could scrape together. They also held a sidewalk sale, to which Joo-Eun contributed colorful silk fabrics and scarves that she had brought with her all those many years ago from Korea. That was back when her dreams were as bright and filled with colorful hope as the fabrics. Those dreams had turned from Technicolor to gray, so why not get rid of the reminders of lost dreams?

Tommy sold his dog-eared stack of comic books and gave Elle the money. He had managed to escape her hooks, but he knew that if she hung around much longer, he would be sucked into her vortex of seduction, manipulation and ambition and might never break free. All he wanted out of life was to be left alone, to maybe get a decent job above ground and a decent woman to be by his side. He wanted no part in the under tow of the household's swirling waters.

All together they managed to purchase Elle's one-way bus ticket, a new outfit from Baker's Department Store, a striped cardboard suitcase, and had given her an extra twenty dollars for spending money. They were rightly proud of themselves and the hugs and tears shed at the bus station were genuine and heart felt. Even Joo-Eun knew that she would miss her daughter's company and her help around the house. Elle had a bright and energetic presence that gave the home an electric tension that was palpable; her loss would be felt by everyone.

"All west bound passengers please place all bags on the loading ramp, have your tickets ready, and begin boarding immediately," the bus driver announced.

Elle gave her brother and parents one last hug, carefully placed her new suitcase on the ramp, and excitedly stepped aboard the big bus. She selected a seat toward the rear so she would have maximum privacy, and settled in for the long trip.

She peered out the dusty, streaked window to wave goodbye but her little family had already left.

"Huh, didn't take them long to get shed of me," she said.

The endless hours aboard a series of buses were spent reading, chatting happily with fellow passengers, and studying for the tests that she knew stood between being admitted to Darlington School and being sent back to Pulaski.

The road whined beneath the big tires, the bus rocked gently back and forth, and strangers came and went from the bus like characters in a Faulkner novel.

Before she knew it, the driver was announcing the stop for Birmingham's downtown station, and Elle stood, gathered her purse and books, and stepped down into a dingy bus terminal. The air was hot and filled with stifling exhaust fumes, and the floors were littered with old newspapers and other trash. She even spotted several puddles of vomit which nearly sent her retching, but she managed to control the urge to heave her greasy biscuit breakfast and candy bar lunch.

As she stood waiting for her suitcase to be pulled from the belly of the bus, she heard someone calling her name.

"Elle Corday," yelled the black man in the liveried uniform, "Elle Corday, please raise your arm!"

She waved to the man, wondering who on earth he could be.

"Well, there you are, Miss," he said, smiling and revealing a mouth filled with large, sparkling white teeth. "I was beginning to believe you had missed your bus."

"No, we just arrived. I'm waiting on my suitcase. Who are you?"

"My name is Sam. The McFarland Foundation folks has sent me to fetch you to the offices, Miss. You jus' wait right here and I'll get your case. What color it is?"

Oh, my God, this is so fabulous she thought, but she said "Well, how nice. Thank you, Sam. It's blue with a darker blue stripe."

Soon they were out of the foul smelling bus terminal and on their way through the hilly green streets of Birmingham. This was Elle's first ride in the luxury of leather seats and air conditioning; the sleek Lincoln Town Car was impressive and she felt like a movie star.

Sam wheeled the big car up a wide circular driveway lined with evergreen trees and pink crepe myrtle bushes, and stopped in front of a white pillared colonial mansion. There was a small brass plaque above the door that read "McFarland Foundation, Est. 1959".

Not having a clue what to do, Elle stayed seated as Sam got out, came around, and opened her door.

"Step right on out, Miss. We here. You go on inside and I'll bring your bag along."

A dumpling of a housekeeper appeared at the door, holding it open for her. She had on a uniform that matched Sam's, only hers was a dress.

For a moment Elle just stood, rooted to the spot, tempted to jump back in the car and tell Sam to take her back to the bus station. That was a world she could recognize. It was disgusting, but understandable. This world of fancy cars, servants in uniforms, and stately mansions was like visiting a foreign country. It was exciting, but very frightening and intimidating. She was beginning to be sorry she had set her sights so high.

Sam sensed her fear and stepped beside her.

"Don't worry, Miss. They real nice inside. Nice folks. Nothin'atall to be skeered of. You just go on in now. Maybelle will show you the way. Just follow her. I'll be right along."

Elle took a deep breath and decided that maybe this place was better after all than that God awful bus station. What did she have to lose?

She followed Maybelle into a broad hallway flanked by elegantly appointed parlors. Both, she noticed, had fireplaces with gilded mirrors hanging over them and lush draperies and sparkling chandeliers. As Maybelle led her further down the hallway to a bookshelf-lined study of some sort, she decided right then and there that she would live in a house like this one day.

"I will," she said aloud. "I definitely will."

She was startled by a female voice behind her.

"You will what, my dear?"

Elle spun around to face the voice.

"Sorry if I startled you. You must be Elle Corday," the woman said. "I'm Dorothy Statler, administrator of the McFarland Foundation. Have a seat, won't you?"

Elle sat on the edge of a brown leather wing back chair, crossed her ankles as she had been taught (by whom she couldn't remember), and clutched her small cloth purse in her lap.

Dorothy Statler sat down behind a large mahogany desk that was bare except for one file sitting starkly in the center. Elle noted that it had her name on it in black ink.

"Welcome to Birmingham, Elle. It is very nice to meet you. We here at the foundation are pleased to be able to offer you assistance with your schooling at Darlington. After we take care of some preliminary items and some paper work, you will be transferred to Rome, Georgia and you may reside either with your sponsors there or in the dormitory facilities. That decision we will leave up to you and Mr. and Mrs. Ted Moore, your sponsors."

This was the first Elle had heard about sponsors.

"Sponsors? I'm confused. I didn't know I was going to have sponsors. Who are they?"

"Nothing to worry about, my dear," Mrs. Statler replied, opening the file folder and shuffling some papers around. "It's a perfectly normal procedure. We here at the foundation provide all the funding, but as a residential student from out of state, and quite young and inexperienced, we prefer that a student such as yourself have the benefit of adult guidance and counseling. The Moores will provide that. They have sponsored students for us before and you will find them quite wonderful. Do you have any other questions?"

Without giving Elle a chance to answer what was apparently a rhetorical question, she continued, "Good. I will have Maybelle show you to your room then. She will also bring you some supper. Tomorrow morning we will begin the testing to make sure you qualify for Darlington School. I'm sure you will pass with flying colors."

With no further ado, Mrs. Statler left the room, her heavy black shoes clacking on the polished heart pine floors.

Elle had visions of being stuck in a basement and having a bowl of gruel for dinner, but she was pleasantly surprised by a third floor corner room with a view of the gardens. Although apparently decorated by someone around a hundred years old and entirely unsuitable for a high spirited teenager, the bed was large and comfortable and the room had its own tiny bathroom attached.

She was in heaven and her dreams of future wealth were reinvigorated. The girl who was too awkward and unusual looking to have a boyfriend, the girl who was considered too low class to be a cheerleader, would be mistress of a manor such as this one day she pledged, and this time no one overheard her.

The bus ride from Birmingham to Rome, Georgia and the lush campus of Darlington School was a breeze after enduring the hardship of the long journey from West Virginia.

Elle had only spoken to her parents once to let them know she was safe. Mrs. Statler had turned out to be rather kind, even though her back was ramrod stiff and her nose was permanently pointed toward the clouds. She had allowed Elle to make the long distance call without making it collect.

Joo-Eun had answered and sounded as though she genuinely missed her daughter. Elle believed her when she said, "House not same without you, Ellie. Nobody smile anymore."

Thoughts of Virginia seemed far behind her now, as the taxi pulled up to the home of her sponsors. Not quite as palatial as the McFarland Foundation, there was still plenty to gasp over as Elle stepped from the cab and was greeted by another housekeeper in a black and white uniform.

"Good afternoon, miss. My name is Coramae. Come with me now."

The home of Theodore and Rita Moore was a wrap-around porch Victorian, with three floors of gingerbread trim, balconies, turrets, and a beautiful gazebo with a cupola on the front lawn. A giant, ancient magnolia tree guarded the home from center front and was in full bloom; its dinner plate sized white flowers gave the air a sweet smell that defined southern charm.

"Miss Rita be with you in a minute, sugar," said Coramae, offering Elle a seat in the exquisite foyer. She sat her suitcase down next to her and couldn't help but feel dowdy in this giant doll house.

Coramae left her alone and Elle took the opportunity to check herself out in a large gold framed triple mirror above the largest buffet table she had ever seen.

My whole family could fit in there she thought, smoothing her bangs and straightening her skirt. She felt wrinkled and dirty from the bus trip and taxi ride and hoped she didn't look as ill kempt as she felt. Her worries were soon erased.

"My my, aren't you just the pretty one," said Rita Moore, introducing herself and welcoming Elle. "How tall are you my dear?"

"Um, five-eight, Miz Moore. Thank you."

"And such beautiful hair. I expect we'll need to see about getting you some skirts that aren't quite so short and perhaps a hair cut. But let's get you settled in and we'll talk about such things later. You can meet my husband Theodore and my daughter Suzanne, if she blesses us with her presence. She's in college now and rarely deems us fit company." Rita Moore smiled, took Elle's hand, and led her up a winding staircase.

She opened the door to a room that in Elle's opinion looked like the pages of a storybook come to life. It was sweet, charming, and very childish. Everything was pink, with miles of lace, rosebuds, angels, cornices and dozens of ornate dolls. There was a large double bed, however, and a decent sized desk for homework so it wasn't a total horror.

She managed a smile. "This is lovely, Miz Moore. I'm sure I'll be very comfortable."

"Well, this was my daughter's room until she moved into the dorms.

When she comes home on weekends she just sleeps in the basement rec' room on the couch or one of the guest rooms. Feel free to put the dolls away if they bother you. Ted, my husband, says they should stay in this room since they were part of our daughter's childhood, but I think that's just plain silly."

"Thank you, Ma'am. What time shall I be ready for dinner?"

"Seven sharp, dear. Just come down and explore, make yourself at home whenever you're ready. Or you can unpack and take a nap. I'll see you at seven if not before. If you need anything, just press that buzzer by the door and Coramae or one of the other colored girls will come and help you. Bye for now." She kissed Elle on the cheek and rushed out the door, trailing a scent of rose water behind her.

By supper time, which Elle found out was what they called the evening meal in Georgia - dinner was a big meal in the middle of the day - she had showered, changed into a pair of Levi denims and a form fitting white tee shirt, and taken a walk through the gardens. She had even managed a short nap in the porch swing and was starving.

Mr. Moore, who insisted she call him Ted, sat at the head of the table and expertly carved the beef roast. Another member of the house staff that he called Sally served browned potatoes, green beans, yeast rolls, and then brought out banana pudding for dessert.

Elle was enjoying the meal so much - it was the first decent meal she had enjoyed in ages without the skimpy portions of rice and boney fish her mother served up - she barely spoke. She smiled when it seemed appropriate, nodded her head, and gave one word answers to the many questions posed by her host and hostess. Their daughter, Suzanne, never showed and her chair sat empty; her place setting paying silent tribute to her parent's empty nest.

As Sally poured after dinner coffee for the Moores, Elle wiped her mouth with the crisp white linen napkin, and burped softly. She hoped they hadn't noticed.

"So, Elle, are you looking forward to beginning school at Darlington next week?" Ted asked.

"Yes sir, I am. This is a dream come true for me. I thought I might never get out of Pulaski, Virginia but it seems that sometimes dreams do come true. The McFarland Foundation, and the kindness of you and Miz Moore, has really given me hope."

"What would you like to study after Darlington?"

"I want to be a lawyer," she replied without hesitating. "I've been reading a lot about the law and how lawyers help people who are in trouble. That's what I want to do."

"Hmmmm," Ted Moore replied. "Well, that means not only college but law school you know. Could be a long haul. Lots of women don't make it in this man's world. Besides, a pretty young thing like you should consider modeling or fashion design. Something a little more lady like than dealing with criminals."

"I'm not pretty enough to be a model, sir. But I'll work hard. You'll see that I will study and do whatever it takes to succeed. What ever it takes," she repeated slowly. "I never let anything stand in my way when I want something."

"Well, I think we've grilled this young lady enough for one evening," said Rita, standing and ringing the bell for the servants. Something about the way her husband was talking to Elle had flashed a warning sign in her subconscious. "Good night, dear. You may go to your room now. Breakfast is at seven. If you miss it you may ask Cook to prepare something for you in the kitchen."

Ted dutifully followed his wife out of the dining room and Elle went upstairs, presenting a pretty view of her rear end in the tight jeans to the secretly watching Ted Moore. The trademark Levis label had never looked so good, undulating up and down with the movement of her hips.

Is she aware of her sexuality, he wondered? *She may only be sixteen, but damn . . .*

"Rita," he called out. "Rita, come on upstairs, honey bunch. I'll rub your back."

Chapter 6

The Darlington Darlings

After a week of reading novels and movie star magazines, taking long walks in the gardens, talking to the kitchen help, and trying to avoid Ted's piercing gazes, Elle found Darlington School everything she had dreamed of and more.

The campus was lush, green, and beautiful, with stately brick buildings and curved walkways. Students chatted in clusters, rode bicycles from dorms to classes, and smiled in the friendly open way that the antebellum South is famous for.

Her classes had been chosen ahead of time, apparently by her sponsors, so all she had to do was register, pick up her books, and then follow the pre-assigned schedule. There was English literature, geometry, world history, biology, religions of the world, and physical education. At PE she found that she had a choice of basketball, golf, volleyball, or softball, and she quickly chose basketball since it seemed the least intimidating. She had never been on a golf course in her life, as far as she knew Pulaski didn't even have one, nor had she ever played volleyball.

Most of the students were friendly, cheerful and welcoming, but there was one clique of girls that seemed jealous or threatened by Elle's beauty and newly found talents on the basketball court. She got a lot of attention from the boys in her shorts and halter top; apparently too much attention to suit some of the girls.

The exercise, a growth spurt, and the hearty meals at the Moore home had proven to be a recipe for a burgeoning voluptuousness that had turned the once tall and gangly Elle into a curvaceous, round breasted young woman. She had kept her hair long, but Rita Moore's professional stylist and nail salon had put the finishing touches on a previously rough canvas. Even tied back, her hair frequently escaped its restraints and on several occasions her large breasts nearly escaped theirs. Having to stop and readjust them cost her team points, which didn't make them happy with her. In spite of that, Elle was nothing short of spectacular on the basketball court and had become a valuable member of the girls' team. The fans were thrilled and attendance at the girls' games nearly doubled that year.

Of course, anytime teenage hormones and insecurity are raging, and you mix in the aggression of sports and the elitist attitudes that fester within wealthy enclaves, volatility is a given. Darlington School, for all its professed social graces, rules, and high minded morality, was just such a hot bed.

When more playing time was given to Elle, less playing time was available for her teammate, a brainy, well-muscled junior classman named Sissy Allbritton. Sissy was used to getting plenty of time on the boards, and her parents were both wealthy alumni of the school. She resented this mixed breed slut cutting in on her turf. She raised hell with the coaches but to no avail.

She decided to take matters into her own hands. One day during the noon break from classes, Sissy and her friends gathered on the lawn, sitting cross-legged in a circle beneath an ancient oak tree dripping with silvery moss. Sandwiches, chips and candy bars filled the center of the circle. A pack of Virginia Slims was camouflaged by a large denim purse.

"Guys, we gotta do something about that goddamn Elle Corday," Sissy said. "She seems to not know her place, which should be working in the laundry or something. Now she's trying to horn in on our playing time. Trying to be the star." She made air quotes around 'star' and rolled her eyes dramatically.

"So," replied one member of Sissy's clique, "what should we do?"

"Yeah, what should we do, Sissy?" asked the owner of the cigarettes.

"Beat the snot out of her after school?"

Everyone giggled but Sissy didn't hesitate. She had given this a lot of thought. "Don't be stupid, Mary Margaret. We'd just get in trouble. No, we should start telling everyone that she's preggers. You know the school hates that. They'll throw her slant-eyed Chinese ass out lickety split and we won't have to worry about her hogging court time anymore."

No one dared correct Sissy - Elle of course was of Korean descent, not Chinese. To them it was all the same anyway. If you weren't born and bred below the Mason-Dixon Line you were a foreigner and didn't amount to a hill of shelled butter beans.

Word, of course, got back to Elle that Sissy was pushing hard to get her kicked off the team, or at least reduced to a minor player. The silly rumor was quickly dismissed since Elle frequently walked around the gym locker room naked. She obviously wasn't pregnant.

The war was on though, and Elle had no intention of losing it. She would, as always, do whatever it took to not just stay in place on the ladder, but to move up as often as possible. If others had to be pushed aside, so be it. She wasn't mean, but she wasn't going to back down from a fight. And she wasn't going to tolerate racism as practiced by spoiled little rich girls with brains the size of the little lightening bugs that flashed in the dark Southern nights.

One day Elle went to the girls' student counselor, closed the door, and broke down into sobs. Her shoulders shook prettily and the counselor, Miss Rosenthal, patted her on the head and handed her a tissue.

"What's the problem, my dear? Tell me what's wrong."

"Well, I've been so happy here at Darlington. Being here is a dream come true for me, you know?" Miss Rosenthal nodded and murmured that she did indeed know. She herself had attended the school and had found safe harbor within its manicured hedges for most of her man-free life.

"And I just don't know what to do," said Elle, distraught and bursting into fresh tears.

"Do about what? I must know what's wrong if I'm to help you," responded Miss Rosenthal in her kindly Southern sugar coated voice.

Elle became momentarily distracted by the over-powering smell of gardenias in the office and looked around for the source of the cloying odor. She found it - a tall vase of the white flowers stood on a credenza by the window.

Turning her gaze back upon the anxious counselor, Elle said, "Well, there's this student who has asked me to cheat. She's afraid of failing a test because it will make her ineligible to play sports. And she knows I'm good in math so she asked me to write her up a cheat sheet. I don't want to break the rules but I don't want her to be mad at me either. I just don't know what to do."

As she continued to sob, Miss Rosenthal came from behind her desk to the sofa where Elle was sitting and sat down beside her, placing her arm around Elle's shoulders. Elle leaned her head over and rested it upon Miss Rosenthal's rarely touched breasts, which felt to Elle like lumpy old feather pillows. The spinster gasped when Elle's warm breath washed over her bosom.

She suddenly felt hot and prickly all over and squirmed against the couch cushion. *Get a hold of yourself old girl,* she thought, but instead of standing up, she stroked Elle's hair and shushed her.

"There, there my dear. Everything will be all right. You just tell me who this person is who wishes to break the Darlington honor code and let the school authorities handle it."

Elle nuzzled the 'pillows' and managed to lift her head enough to breathe softly into Miss Rosenthal's ear, nearly sending her into spasms. Somehow Elle possessed finely-tuned radar for people's vulnerabilities and soft spots. Their body language spoke to her nearly as loudly as did their actual voices. She heard the spinster's desperate need to be touched, and intuitively sensed a cauldron of passion long buried beneath her print dresses and large knee-length underpants.

"But, Miss Rosenthal, she'll know it was me that told. She and her friends, they play basketball with me. They will make my life miserable." She dropped her head back down on the pretext of new tears, sending waves of hot breath over the lacy neckline of the floral silk dress.

"No, no. No one will know where the information came from, I can assure you. Don't you worry. I'll handle everything very discreetly."

"Oh, that would be wonderful, Miss Rosenthal. Just wonderful. Thank you so much. Would it be okay if I come back from time to time and talk to you? You are so kind."

"Of course, dear. Come back anytime. I might even have you over to my apartment for a nice meal one evening. How would that be?"

"Terrific. Just let me know and I'm there," replied Elle. "And, by the way, the girl's name is Sissy Allbritton."

Elle stood, seemingly accidentally brushing her hand across Miss Rosenthal's thigh, kissed her softly on the cheek, thanked her again for everything, and slipped out the door. By the time she reached the hallway she was smiling, and Miss Rosenthal had gone into her private powder room to freshen up a bit.

"My, what a precocious child," she said to herself in the mirror. "But I certainly hope she comes to me again soon for counseling. Sweet dear. I'm quite certain I can help her."

One week later Sissy was a no show at basketball practice and after a brief but enigmatic announcement, Elle asked the coach where she really was.

"Don't know," she said. "Her parents just called and said she was not going to be playing any more this year. Guess that means more time for you, eh Corday?"

"Yeah, Coach, I guess so. Put me in. I'm ready!"

She impressed the coach by suggesting the team gather in a circle and pray for Sissy.

Chapter 7

Nothing in Life is Free

After what Elle came to think of as the 'Sissy Incident', her life at Darlington School was idyllic in most ways.

Her grades were always in the top two percentile, and she was the undisputed star of the girls' basketball team. She also had a boyfriend. During the week she lived in a dorm room, sharing a small room with one other girl. Her roommate was a quiet freshman who rarely spoke to the exotic Elle. She was afraid of her, intimidated by her, wanted desperately to be like her and knew she never could be, so she just tried to concentrate on her studies and ignore her roommate as best she could.

When Elle came into the room, which was not often, she put headphones on and stared into a thick text book or garish horror novel, usually just lifting a hand in a silent wave hello.

Elle's boyfriend was a blonde, handsome senior classman who worshipped the ground she walked on. He loved her with the desperation that only raging hormones can generate, and thought about her constantly. Kyle dreaded his spring graduation because he was from Kansas and knew that his destiny was to travel thousands of miles west. His future in Emporia, Kansas managing his father's furniture business did not include Elle. His born-again parents would have a heart attack at the sight of her. She reeked sexuality in subtle ways that they would neither be able to pinpoint, understand, or tolerate. He could only imagine, if she was this beautiful and desirable at sixteen, what she would be like all grown up. He had only managed to get so far as to nibble at her breasts and put his hands in her pants; beyond that she pushed him away, ordering him to stop.

He lived for the day, could think of nothing else, when she would allow him to 'put it in'. His roommate was getting tired of hearing him grunting and groaning while masturbating to pictures in *Playboy Magazine*. He spent every penny of extra money buying her little gifts: bouquets of flowers from the grocery store cooler, cheap jewelry, and cute stuffed animals. Nothing helped but he kept trying. One day, soon he hoped, he would find the right key to unlock her tightly closed legs. Something had to work or he was going to go blind; at least that's what the other guys kept warning him against.

On weekends, which began at the end of classes on Friday afternoon, a car and driver would pick Elle up and she would be driven to the Moore mansion and her dollhouse room. She had managed to, one by one, stash the dolls away in boxes, under the bed, and in closets, but she couldn't convince Mr. or Mrs. Moore to redecorate the room. They thought it was perfect the way it was. One chilly evening during Elle's first Christmas in Rome, Elle found out why.

Saturday had dawned with bright blue skies and temperatures in the forties, which Elle found wonderful after the much harsher Virginia winters. She spent the day shopping with Mrs. Moore, then wrapping gifts in the cozy den. They trimmed the tree, sipped hot chocolate with mounds of tiny marshmallows, and laughed together like old friends. Suzanne had chosen to spend the holidays with friends at their Sugar Loaf Mountain ski chalet, so Elle was center stage in the family festivities. She didn't mind, secretly suspecting that she would benefit by receiving lots of gifts that might have gone to the wayward and absent daughter.

After a long hot bubble bath, Elle got into bed with her favorite book - a courtroom legal thriller - and soon was fast asleep under the floral quilt. She dreamed about getting her college diploma, her parents and brother whistling cheers at her, smiling and proud of her success. She would be the first person in her family to graduate from college. She was going to make tons of money, buy her parents a beautiful home, buy her brother a fancy car, and dress in designer clothes like she drooled over in *Seventeen*

Magazine.

She rolled over, snuggled more deeply into the covers, but suddenly felt the presence of someone in her room. She opened her eyes to find Ted Moore sitting in the white wicker rocking chair, holding one of the baby dolls, rocking silently and smiling at her.

"Sorry, did I wake you?" he said, whispering hoarsely.

"What are you doing?" Elle asked, confused and a bit frightened.

"Just watching you sleep, my dear. I do it often. Sorry to have awakened you this time. Didn't mean to startle you." He continued the gentle rocking, cuddling the baby doll as though it were real. Then Elle noticed that his hand was inside the baby doll's diaper, his finger rubbing the doll back and forth in cadence with the rocking motion of the chair.

Oh, my God, how creepy, she thought. *What should I do?*

She closed her eyes and began taking deep breaths, trying to calm herself. Should she scream for Mrs. Moore? She could see the drama play out as she was sent home to Pulaski, her dreams of college shattered. What would the McFarland Foundation think if she caused a scandal?

"That's right, my dear. Just close your eyes and go back to sleep. Daddy will just sit here for a bit and rock the baby. Babies love Daddy. Do you love Daddy, Elle? Do you?"

"Uh, yeah, I love you. But I'm sleepy. Could you go now?"

"Hmmm, Daddy will go soon, but he has a bit of a problem. Open your eyes and look at Daddy's problem."

She opened one eye to peek, and realized that he had stood up and his slacks were down around his ankles. He had a huge erection - bigger than her father's. It was terrifying in its size. And it was different from her father's in another way, looking like a hooded snake. It was ugly and strange looking to Elle. It was repulsive. She squeezed her eyes shut again.

"Can you help Daddy fix his problem? Elle? Can you be a good girl?"

"I don't know what you want me to do," Elle replied, now crying softly into her pillow. His hoarse whispering was more frightening that the words he was saying. "I'm afraid."

"Now, now, don't be afraid. I'll show you exactly what to do. I won't hurt you."

He sat back down, removed his shoes and slacks, and crawled beneath the childish rose quilt. He was pleased to find Elle nude; his daughter had never slept in the nude. This was a magnificent Christmas gift, all wrapped up in pretty pink flowers.

"Just lie still and let Daddy do all the work," he whispered. "Don't make a sound. We don't want to wake up Mommy. Mommy would be very angry with you if she found out you were naughty, right?"

He pulled Elle tightly against him and began trying to push himself inside her from behind. He pushed repeatedly but her legs were stiff with fear and she was dry and impossible to penetrate.

"Relax, Elle. Open your knees and relax. This will feel good, you'll see."

She managed to spread her legs slightly, but the more he pushed with the large hard erection, the tighter she became. He decided to resort to other measures.

He rolled her onto her back, spread her legs wide, and bent to lick her.

"You are too dry and you're not letting Daddy in," he said. "This will help and make you feel good too."

He continued to lick and suck at her clitoris and in spite of herself, she began to respond, slowly raising her hips to push against his face. She grabbed his hair with both hands and began pushing his head against her. Dryness was no longer a problem.

He lifted his head to catch his breath. "Now that's my girl. You're getting the hang of this."

"Don't stop," she cried, pressing her heels into the bed and pushing herself up toward him.

"No, you're ready for the real thing now," he said, rising up and thrusting himself harshly inside her.

After several forceful thrusts, he exploded inside her, rolled off, and slipped his pants on.

"Remember, this is our little secret. Daddy feels much better now."

He picked up his shoes and slipped out of the room without another word.

Elle, however, felt terrible. She felt dirty, used, and somehow unfulfilled, restless, and empty at the same time.

She managed to fall back to sleep, and when she awoke she nearly believed that it had been a bad dream. Then she saw the baby doll laying on the floor, its tiny pink panties hanging off of one leg, its eyes staring hatefully right at her. Before getting dressed, she kicked it under the bed.

Christmas came and went in a flurry of house warming parties, delicious baked treats provided daily by the kitchen staff, and an array of extravagant gifts from the Moores that would have made a movie star envious.

By the time Elle went back to third semester classes at Darlington, she was rosy cheeked, had gained five pounds, and had an entire new wardrobe of cashmere sweaters, pleated skirts, and a charm bracelet (given to her by Mr. Moore) with miniature baby dolls, rattles, and prams hanging from a solid gold chain.

Mrs. Moore had looked a little curious when Elle had ripped open the signature blue Tiffany jewelry box, but decided it was innocent enough. She had never noticed that Elle had removed all the dolls from her room and preferred to think of her charge as a girl-child, not the teenager she really was. She also didn't notice the sly, playful wink that Mr. Moore directed at Elle as she opened the gift.

Dragging two new Samsonite suitcases packed with her holiday booty, Elle found her dour roommate propped up on her bed, ear phones in place, reading a well-worn edition of *Anna Karenina*.

After placing the suitcases on top of her bed, which was dressed in sophisticated black and white linens and stacked with designer pillows, Elle went over and pulled the ear phones off of Vicky.

"Hey, what are you doing?"

"Listen up, I need to talk to you. Where are you from?" Elle asked the surprised girl.

"I'm from someplace where people leave you alone," she replied, pouting and picking up the headset.

"Sorry," Elle said apologetically. "It's just that I didn't have such a great holiday. I didn't mean to take it out on you. So, where are you from?"

"Athens," the girl said, determined not to drag this conversation out. How dare this bitch, who was gorgeous as all hell and had everything in the world going for her, how dare she invade her space.

"You sure as hell don't look or sound Greek to me."

"Athens, Georgia, crazy. Way east of here. It's nice there."

"Are people crazy and mean there? Is there a college?"

"Yeah, the University of Georgia is there. That makes it kind of open minded, but I guess you'd think the locals were mean. They don't like anybody who's different and not from the all Holy South. My dad went to college in Atlanta, Emory University, and he's always talking about how great it was there. 'Diverse' he says. 'Anything goes there' he says. Like he isn't just another boring member of the Moose and the Elks and any other goddamn animal organization he can find. Anyway, if it's big city fun you're looking for, Atlanta's the place."

"Well," said Elle turning to unpack, "then that's where I'm headed when I finish here. Athens first maybe, then Atlanta, here I come."

The next night Elle had a date with Kyle, who noticed right away that something was different about her. He kept asking, but couldn't get a straight answer as to how her holiday had been, except the standard one word replies like 'fine' and 'nice'.

Elle wore a new outfit for their drive-in movie date; a form fitting cashmere sweater set and the latest thing in designer jeans. The jeans were so tight Kyle thought he could see her pubic mound clearly outlined, but it might have just been his imagination ballooned by a hormonal surge.

Before they had even parked and pulled the speaker into the car, he had an erection that was threatening to bust the zipper on his own jeans.

Elle nibbled at popcorn while Kyle, his arm draped across her shoulder, rubbed her right breast. He didn't think it was possible, but just touching her, even through the thickness of two sweaters and a bra, made him get even bigger. He was in pain.

"Elle," he said, pulling her chin around to look into her eyes, "Elle, you gotta let me do it. You just gotta. Look at me. Look at what you do to me."

He took her hand and placed it on his crotch, inflaming him further and making his mouth go completely dry.

"Kyle, we're not gonna do anything. I've told you and told you. I'm saving myself for marriage. You can touch me if you want to; I think that's okay. Will that help?" She kissed him softly on the lips and rubbed the inside of his thigh.

He reached between her legs and rubbed at her roughly, trying to relieve his painful erection, but the feel of her silky pubic hair and damp warmth only made it worse.

"Oh, God," he whispered. "Oh, God, Elle, you're killing me."

He reached over and released the seat back, giving himself room to maneuver, then pushed Elle forcefully down in the seat. He placed one hand over her mouth and used the other to pull down her jeans.

Elle was furious. How dare this kid, this man-boy, try to force himself on her. She bit his hand and he removed it quickly, but used it to punch her in the face. She felt dizzy and nearly passed out but she realized that he was much stronger than she was, and he was in a frenzy. The last thing she wanted was a big screaming fight scene here at the drive-in where everybody from the school came on their dates. He might kill her, she realized, or really hurt her, and decided that she would be better off to cooperate. At least for the moment.

"You didn't have to hit me you asshole!"

"Well be still. This won't take a minute, but I'm gonna fuck you and fuck you hard so lay back and enjoy it."

In spite of the bulge his erection had made in his jeans, when he entered Elle she realized immediately that he was no where near as large as Ted Moore, a/k/a Daddy. Kyle was indeed no big deal. Not even as big as her father. She was starting to amass some data for comparison purposes.

When he pulled out and zipped up he looked down at her.

"Well, where's all the blood, Miss Virgin? Huh? Thought you were saving it for marriage. What a crock of shit. What a fucking phony you are. From now on, I'll fuck your brains out whenever I want to and you won't do a goddamn thing about it will you?"

"Kyle, I thought you loved me. How can you treat me this way? You're being mean." She tried to whimper and cry but she was still too mad to pull it off.

"And besides, if you pull this stunt again, you will pay. I will tell my sponsors, the Moores, and they are rich enough to make your life a living hell. Especially *Mister* Moore, if you get my drift. He tends to think of me as *his* little girl, so now, take me home so I can wash you away. You make me feel filthy!"

She pulled her jeans up, zipped and snapped them, and squeezed over against the door as far away from him as possible.

Kyle did as he was told and drove her home, suddenly feeling ashamed of himself as he watched her huddle against the door like a frightened mouse. He even tried to kiss her goodnight outside the dorm like they'd had a normal date but she ran inside and slammed the door shut in his face.

Elle had learned a couple of things that night. Sex was a powerful, powerful weapon. And men were very, very weak. She thought about that as she sat up in bed with an ice pack on her jaw. How could she use that information to get rich? Rich and powerful. She knew her body would be a big asset, but she also knew that a good education was her real entry ticket to the powerful enclaves of the rich and famous. She even coined a name for it: Pussy Power.

Chapter 8

A Night To Remember

"Get a shot of that tattoo, Officer," the FBI Agent in Charge told the City of Atlanta Police Department's booking officer.

My friend Jade was being politely ushered through the booking process under her real name, Elle Corday-Whitmire, although she had been roughly strip searched. The matrons in the jail loved taking down the rich and famous a peg or two during the booking process, especially when the brass wasn't looking.

The tattoo in question was small and discreet, but the matron had made a point of showing it to the officers, tracing it with her gloved finger. Had she been alone with the prisoner, she would love to have kissed it. She'd seen a lot of tattoos of course, but she'd never seen one like this.

The image of a child's baby doll was finely drawn in purple ink on a canvas of creamy skin just above the nipple of her left breast. The doll had no eyes, just the words **Pussy Power** written across its face.

After the tattoo had been recorded, purportedly for identification purposes, Jade was placed in a holding cell to await her attorney, who had already been called.

Even though she was a lawyer, only a fool would represent herself, and Jade was no fool. She also didn't want anyone from her own firm to be in charge of her fate. They had been good to her, and had promoted her to senior partner, but she had worked hard for it and she deserved it. They hadn't done her any favors; in fact they had made it a challenge every step of the way. What had finally pushed them over the edge was

an offer from a firm that frequently competed with them for corporate clients: Goldstein, Stevens & Loeb, PC. Besides, they were international and corporate law specialists with no criminal law expertise.

So, she wanted someone from Goldstein, Stevens & Loeb to represent her. She knew they respected her and even though she had chosen to stay with their competition, she had faced them on opposite sides of the courtroom many times and knew they were excellent. They were ethical, competent, and worked hard for the benefit of their clients. She respected them, especially the firm's founder, Richard Goldstein and old Donald Stevens. They were both Atlanta courtroom legends. An added bonus was that as staunch Republicans, they had contributed heavily to her husband's senate campaigns. She just hoped someone would show up soon and end this nightmare. How could such a beautiful evening, the culmination of her career, end so horribly?

She knew Harrison must be fit to be tied; they wouldn't let her talk to him or anyone else. Stu would probably know because he still had lots of contacts in Georgia law enforcement circles, but she couldn't reach out to him either. Following the rules, she got one call and one call only so she made it to a lawyer. They hadn't even told her what she was charged with. *What the hell is going on,* she wondered.

Now, you may be wondering how I am able to convey all this juicy information, seeing as how I wasn't there and all. But don't worry, Sugar, 'cause all that and much more will be revealed soon enough. For now, you just take my word for it that this was a rough night for my employee, friend and lover. I could have told them all about that tattoo, too, for I have kissed it many times trying to make Jade feel better. Sometimes it worked; sometimes it didn't, but I never quit trying.

There was a time when she became enamored of Noir and those two had a thing going for a while, but I knew that was just an infatuation - Noir was fascinated with Jade's extraordinarily fine and tasty body. (I swear, Jade tasted like imported caviar to me and I think Noir thought so too. Fact, I always enjoyed a glass of champagne when we made love. It fizzed deliciously when it hit her warm skin and just seemed to add something

special to the occasion.) Jade was fascinated with Noir because she was black. Jade had never experienced sexual intimacy with a black woman before, especially right after she came to work for me to earn college money. Curiosity licked the 'cat', so to speak.

I counted on that fascination ending and it did in a spectacular fashion, but there I go getting ahead of myself again.

Jade had found an escort agency in the Yellow Pages when she started college. She was looking for part time work that wouldn't interfere with her college classes and figured an escort service (we call them out call services) would be just the ticket. It would offer her decent money and evening hours that would be perfect.

One of the men she 'escorted' from time to time was a retired cop turned private detective named Stu Butler. Stu lived in Atlanta and had offices there, but when he hired girls, he liked to get them from Athens. He liked the college girls he said, because they weren't dumb. They also had stars in their eyes and futures planned so they weren't likely to be crazy as hell or ruin his marriage. Although his frumpy wife didn't satisfy him in the bedroom, she was a super star in the kitchen.

Stu was a big rumpled sort of a man, hair always a mess, three days growth of beard was the usual, and he always, and I mean always, worn a shoulder holster with his favorite weapon shoved tightly inside. You might say he was a typical Georgia gun nut, but a kinder way might be to say he was an avid collector. He once told me he had a gun room in his Sandy Springs trailer home with over a hundred hand guns and twenty or thirty long guns.

His favorite gun, though, and the one always either on his night stand or strapped to his large body was a Desert Eagle .50 AE with a custom IonFusion Tiger Sharp finish. The gun was huge, intimidating, and he thought it suited his three-hundred pound bulk better than some small pistol.

After about a year of seeing Jade on a fairly regular basis, Stu got to be very fond of her. So fond, in fact, that he was concerned about her safety with the out-call business. Jade had a way of getting under the skin of

her customers, much like she had gotten under mine. There was a sweet innocence and vulnerability about her. You wanted to take care of her, make her happy, and before you knew it you were hooked.

"You're eventually gonna meet up with a nut case," he told her, "or catch some kinda fuckin' disease, which you will then give to me."

"Well don't sugar coat it," Jade had replied, laughing. "What do you want me to do? Marry you and live happily ever after? Make a bunch of little redneck babies to run around with toy guns and shoot at the black children?"

"I got a wife, honey. Besides, you don't cook and I love my greens and grits too much to give that up." He rubbed his big belly for emphasis, then he told her about my in-call business in Atlanta.

"Roxy's got a nice place up there in Buckhead. I'm sure she'd let you come up there and work part time. You'll make more money and be better taken care of. You gotta promise you'll take care of me too though, when my little soldier needs some lovin'."

Wasn't long after that conversation that she did meet up with a nut. Guy got stuck on her and followed her around campus like a sick puppy until she had to call the campus cops on him. When they arrested him he had a huge Bowie knife in his backpack and a record a lot longer than his dick.

That was when she came to me, gave her name as Jade, and the rest, as they say, is history. Stu could never remember to call her Jade, though, which is how I initially found out she had given me a bogus name. No big deal. Most of my girls use fake names, kind of like strippers do.

Jade and Noir were the backbone of my business, even though I had plenty of other girls to fill out my roster of pleasure. Many of them, as I mentioned before, were college students and I always kept a few bored housewives on the payroll. Suburban housewives from places like Lawrenceville, Alpharetta and Mableton are valuable in the escort business for a couple of reasons. First, they are at least somewhat experienced in the sack. Second, they are rarely satisfied in their home bedrooms, so they are adventurous when it comes to love making, and they generally enjoy it.

And third, they know how to keep their mouth shut because they have a lot to lose. They also tend not to get emotionally involved with the clients, or 'fall in love' like the younger girls do. They just do their thing and go home to hubby and the kids. It's just a job to them, even if it's a rather unusual and exciting one. It pays a hell of a lot better than selling makeup from a magazine too.

The world is truly a funny place. You got men coming to professional hookers to get laid because their wives are too tired or too busy to fuck them. Then you got housewives working as hookers because their husbands can't make them come. I reckon the ass is always greener on the other side of the bed.

And just to round out the pussy menu, I had a fat girl 'cause some men get off on searching for the pussy in the fat rolls, a midget girl, and a girl, swear to God, with a third boob. Sounds circus-like I know, but you gotta meet the demands of your clientele. And my clientele were some of Atlanta's richest and most prominent, but they had tastes and desires for the strangest things, including being dominated and peed on. Bad part of hiring the freakier girls was having to audition them, so sometimes I cheated. I had them audition each other and I watched on the discreetly hidden cameras.

I had rooms and equipment and girls to cater to most any whim, but to make sure my girls stayed safe I had Stu install an elaborate electronic surveillance and taping system. Not only could I watch what was going on in any room, I could record it at the touch of a button. I could also, if I was busy, set certain rooms to record automatically. The equipment was even voice-activated so we didn't just waste tape on empty rooms. Stu did a helluva good job setting up all the hidden cameras and equipment for me, I have to give him that. I know the sex business backwards and forwards but electronics is not my thing. He also wired my private offices so I could create a diary of sorts in case I ever needed evidence or proof of any kind.

No one but me and Stu knew about my systems. I never told Jade or any of the girls because I didn't want them to get paranoid, or to play to the cameras. If you start doing that, your client is going to catch on and know they're being taped. And no client wants that, believe me. Especially the members of law enforcement, uptight Republicans or the preachers. Oh, honey, we get 'em all at *Hot'lanta Belles*.

-Chapter 9-

Sin'ator Whitmire

Senator Harrison T. Whitmire III was indeed fit to be tied. He paced the filthy tile floor of downtown Atlanta's city police department booking center, desperate to see his wife. The Federal booking center in the historic Richard B. Russell Building was closed after 6:00 p.m. and all booking and holding was done in off hours by the City of Atlanta. The place was a human zoo.

Harrison wasn't particularly worried about Elle, after all she was a lawyer and capable of looking out for herself, but he desperately wanted to know what in the hell was going on. This was shaping up to be a nightmare. Newspaper reporters regularly hung around the booking center at night and on weekends hoping for a celebrity scoop. Not that they would have to work very hard. The whole thing had been witnessed by reporters at the reception so he new satellite trucks and a full media blitz were only minutes away. He was hoping to get Elle out and home before that happened.

Senator Whitmire's district was extremely conservative, and as a staunch Republican he had been elected on a 'back to family values' platform. His opponent had been beaten handily after being caught in a cock fighting sting. The Georgia Bureau of Investigation had been there, filming the whole thing, and when the former Senator Barksdale had been clearly seen throwing money down on a big red cock, the G.B.I. blocked the doors and arrested everyone in the barn.

PETA and the Humane Society had donated money to Whitmire's campaign and run ads on television and radio. Whitmire's family had a huge horse ranch, *Cherokee Falls,* located on three hundred rolling acres in Cherokee County. The ranch was famous for its racing stock and Kentucky born breeding stallion. The beautiful pastures, bucolic setting, and miles of white fencing were made for television.

Pictures of Elle and Harrison walking down a red clay ranch road, a black stallion between them tossing his mane in the wind, sealed the deal. Family values, a beautiful wife, a solid Georgia pedigree, and true animal lovers were an unbeatable combination. Barksdale didn't stand a whore's chance in heaven of being re-elected.

And now with less than two years to go before another election, Harrison's beautiful, exotic wife was sitting behind bars charged with God knows what. And of course the press at the reception would make sure the event was covered in the Atlanta Journal-Constitution on both the society and the business pages.

Now it would probably be on the front page instead; Elle hand cuffed and being led away like some common criminal. And then reporters would start digging into his past and his family's past and trying to find skeletons. Not that there were any that he was aware of, but every family has its share of dumb cousins so there was probably something ugly lurking in someone's closet.

This shit just didn't happen to upstanding Republicans. Did it?

He thought for a moment about how much he loved her.

They had met at a Republican fund raiser at the Marriott Marquis while she was still attending law school at Emory University. He had no idea why she had come - she was obviously not a political animal or he would have met her sooner - but from the moment he saw her standing near the ballroom window looking for all the world like an oriental figurine he knew he had to have her. Not in the carnal sense of having, but in the proprietary way men own fine horses and beautiful watches. He had to *have* her. She would be his if it was the last thing he would do.

After interrupting her conversation with one of his primary election rivals, virtually pushing the much shorter man aside, Harrison introduced himself and asked her to marry him.

"Sure," she replied quickly. "Let's go find a Justice of the Peace shall we?"

"Well, maybe not this minute. I don't even know your name. But someday I will marry you."

"My name is Elle Corday," she said, shaking his hand. "One of my law professors suggested I attend tonight. I will be looking for work in the not too distant future and if I'm not mistaken, there are a few attorneys here." Her brilliant smile made his heart thud.

That night began a courtship that lasted until Elle's graduation from Emory. Beginning with a ride home from the reception, Harrison began a slow campaign of wining and dining, determined to lead up to their marriage.

Elle too sensed the importance of the potential relationship. She did her homework, as usual, and discovered that he was from a prominent family and she scouted *Cherokee Falls*, deciding that no matter how she ended up feeling about the man, his horse ranch was spectacular. She wanted it. To go from a three-room clapboard house in Pulaski, Virginia to the colonial mansion at the ranch was a vivid real life embodiment of her dreams. If only those mean children could see her sitting astride a beautiful Paso Fino horse doing its elegant quick-step corto gait! What delicious revenge that would be.

She deliberately kept the courtship at a slow pace, teasing him with glimpses and touches of her body, but only after a full six months of dating, during which he presented her with increasingly valuable gifts, did she allow him to make love to her.

They packed a picnic lunch and had ridden to the farthest corner of the ranch property; a hidden meadow by a trickling stream, surrounded by pecan trees and blackberry bushes.

Harrison tied his roan gelding and her favorite little bay mare to a tree stump and spread a plaid woolen blanket on the ground. The cook had provided them with a bottle of cabernet, a loaf of French bread, several savory cheeses, marinated olives, and thinly sliced country ham, which they devoured. They laughed at silly jokes and fed each other the dessert of chocolate dipped blackberries, kissing each other's palms and licking the gooey chocolate from their fingertips.

"Elle, you are driving me crazy," he said, gesturing toward the bulge in his English riding breeches.

She laughed, and replied, "You ain't seen nothin' yet, Senator," and pulled her top off over her head, revealing a pale pink lacy bra that was designed with cut outs for her tempting nipples. This was also his first view of the tattoo.

He leaned closer, tracing the enigmatic baby doll with his finger, then he rubbed her nipples with the palms of his hands. He reached behind her to unsnap the bra, tossing it aside as she lay down on the blanket and pulled his head down so that he could suckle at her breast.

After a moment, he lifted his head and asked her, "Tell me about the tattoo? What does that mean? Pussy Power?"

"Harrison, it means what it says. My whole life I have struggled to achieve power. The power a child doesn't have in an adult world. The power a woman doesn't have in a man's world. And every time I find that when it gets right down to it, what I have between my legs provides all the power I need." *And you'll soon see that's true* she thought.

"Did someone hurt you as a child?" he asked, suddenly concerned and feeling protective.

"Many times," she said, suddenly looking very sad and distant, as though long buried memories were pushing their way up and into their beautiful day. She had a momentary flash of the scrawny child, ragged bangs hiding a dirty face, so desperate for love that she seduced her own father.

She had never told anyone about those episodes of school peer rejection, nor about watching her parents making love and copying the acts, but for reasons that she could not explain, she told all of it to Harrison that day.

He listened quietly, never interrupting, but when she finished, he kissed her eyes, licked away her tears, and vowed that no one would ever hurt her again.

"No more," he said. "There will be nothing but happiness for you from now on. Any one who even thinks about hurting you will have to go through me and the United States government. If your father weren't already dead, I would kill him!"

"Oh, Harrison, thank you for listening. I hope I haven't shocked you to your sweet Southern core." Smiling, the old Elle is back and in control, she added, "Now that you've heard all about it, would you like to see my powerful pussy?"

His answer was a soft kiss and a groan, which she took as a yes. The horses watched through big lazy brown eyes as their riders rolled around in the soft Georgia grass, sealing a deal that would secure one's future and one's downfall.

Six months after their romantic picnic, Harrison presented Elle with a huge cushion cut center stone diamond ring accented with what seemed like hundreds of sparkling miniature diamonds and asked her to be his wife. The twelve carat wedding set had been in his family for generations and his mother, after meeting Elle only once, readily agreed to the use of her own mother's engagement ring. It had always seemed just 'too much' for her to wear, but felt it suited Elle's lovely lithe fingers to a tee. She remained skeptical about the woman her son had chosen, but after receiving a harsh rebuke for even questioning his love and the woman's integrity, she had dropped the subject. His mind was obviously made up and she didn't want to risk alienating him further.

Elle had said "Yes, I will marry you Harrison. And I will try very hard to make you happy." If he noticed that she didn't pledge her love, he said nothing. He would take whatever she could give, and accept it gratefully.

"Every breath you take makes me very happy, my dear. I need nothing more."

"Ahhh, stated like a true politician," she replied, but kissed him deeply to seal the deal.

Just one more rung up the ladder, she thought, but nearly losing her balance when he told her how much he wanted children. Was she ready for that?

Since their wedding, she had brought passion and beauty into his very serious life and made him feel that life was indeed worth living. His entire life he'd had everything a person could want, but his parents were busy, cold, and distant. When Elle was wrapped around him or when he was pushed deeply inside her, he was happy and filled with a new kind of joy he'd never known before. He also knew that she didn't love him; not nearly the way he loved her, but that was okay too. As long as she stuck with him, stayed by his side, he could face anything. He would take on all comers, defeat any enemy, to keep her in his bed and close to his heart. Whether or not she loved him was irrelevant. She needed him for some reason, and that was good enough.

He blinked away the memories and was relieved to see attorney Irving Loeb walk in through the double glass doors and pass through the security check and metal detectors, snapping his thoughts back to the problems at hand. Harrison had met Loeb only once, at a Republican fund raiser, but he liked him a lot. He had apparently been relaxing at home when he got the call from Elle; he was wearing a Nike jogging suit and coordinating sparkling white tennis shoes that had obviously never seen a tennis court.

"Irving, good to see you. Thanks for coming so quickly," Harrison said, offering his hand to the small, bespectacled attorney.

"Hello, Harrison. How's Elle? What's going on? She sounded quite distraught when she called and didn't tell me much."

"Shit, Irv, I've got no idea. We were at a reception at the High Museum to celebrate Elle's new partnership deal and the fucking FBI showed up and hauled her away like a common goddamn criminal. Excuse my language, but I'm about to lose my fucking mind! How dare they?"

"Calm down, Harrison, we'll get to the bottom of this. Could be a case of mistaken identity or something simple to clear up. Let me go back and see her. We'll regroup and figure out a plan after I talk to Elle. I assume coming up with bail money is not a problem?"

"Of course bail is no problem. I'll pay whatever it takes. I just want her safely back in my arms, Irv. This is ridiculous!" *And out of camera range* he thought, then immediately felt guilty for even letting those selfish thoughts slip into his consciousness.

Loeb assured him that she would be released soon, if not on her own recognizance then on bail. Surely they weren't going to play hard ball with this hot potato. Make her stay put until a bond hearing could be arranged. That could take forty-eight hours. He knew the FBI and the GBI were both masters at playing games with jurisdictions, venues, moving the prisoner around and 'losing' the paperwork, but unless they were all suicidal they wouldn't do it with such a high profile arrestee.

Loeb's first stop was at the booking desk.

"I'd like to see my client please. Elle Corday-Whitmire. And I'd like to know what, if anything, she's been charged with."

"You can see your client, sir. I'll have an officer show you back to her holding cell. As it stands right now, she's been charged with conspiracy to murder, tax fraud, tax evasion, money laundering, violations of the Rico Act, and felony assault with intent to do bodily harm. Due to the interstate jurisdictional issues, the Federal Bureau of Investigation is involved as well."

Holy shit, Loeb thought. *What the hell has she done?*

Chapter 10

One Mother of a Summer

Elle didn't officially break up with Kyle after he forced himself on her at the drive-in movie, she just never spoke to him again. If she ran into him on campus she looked right through him, as though he were invisible. If he spoke she didn't hear. He ceased to exist for her and that somehow punished him worse than a screaming break up fight would have.

He felt guilty and would have welcomed her rage, swallowed her venom with relish, and done almost anything to win her back. He tried to call her. She hung up. He wrote her notes; she ripped them to shreds and tossed them away unread. And not that it would have made him feel any better, but he never knew that his actions had changed her in a way that none of her other abusers had. His brutal rape of her, his taking forcefully what should have been hers to give, had made her realize that she had power.

Between her legs lay a powerful force of nature - a secret weapon. And she had decided that she would use that power to control her destiny, secure her future, and make herself invincible. She would give it way, sell it, or keep it chaste, according to her own wishes. No one would ever force themselves between her legs again. After all, she figured, if what she had down there was so desirable, so special, so downright juicy and delicious, men should be willing to pay for the privilege of looking at it, touching it, kissing it, or entering it. And pay they would. She didn't know how yet, but she knew she had something of supreme value and she would use it wisely.

She spent hours with a small compact makeup mirror, her legs spread wide, looking at herself so that she could fully understand her allure. She wanted to see what men saw. She also wanted to know what felt good and what didn't and so she also spent time with creams and various objects, especially her own fingers, pleasuring herself. She bought a larger, full length mirror which she hung on the wall opposite her bed, so that she could watch herself come to the strumming of her own oiled fingers. She knew other girls partially shaved their pussies, she had seen them in the locker rooms and dorm hallway, but she decided she didn't want to do that. Instead, she brushed and combed her pubic hair so that it was lustrous and full. She kept herself meticulously clean and fresh smelling; after all, this was her power. She loved looking at herself, touching herself, and eventually completely understood why others did too.

One night after Ted Moore had satisfied himself, she mentioned to him that his manhood was much larger than her boyfriend's. He made her explain to him what had happened with Kyle, how she knew about his penis, and after telling him about the rape she assured him that she wasn't seeing Kyle any more. When Ted left her room, he had a troubled and angry look on his face that made Elle feel as though he was on her side and would protect her against predators like Kyle. After all, no feral predator likes competition; Elle was just learning how to play the game of pitting the men in her life against each other for her own benefit.

Toward the end of her senior year at Darlington School, Elle suddenly realized that she had missed a period. Pin pricks of fear dotted her forehead and she broke out into a sweat. *Oh, God, could I be pregnant?*

She had no idea what to do. Who could she ask?

The only person she was allowing to enter her secret power dome as she now thought of it, was Ted Moore. He slipped quietly into her bed about once a month, did his business and left without a word. He always left a small piece of jewelry on her night stand and she had amassed quite a nice collection of gold and silver bracelets, anklets, and earrings. Whenever Rita asked her where she got the new baubles she told her that her family had sent them to her or they were from her boyfriend. Rita doubted if that was true but had no way to prove otherwise and sensed that she shouldn't pry too hard.

Elle decided to go to the student clinic; they would be bound by patient confidentiality rules wouldn't they? She hoped so. And their services were free of charge to students.

After filling out forms, providing a urine sample, and waiting for hours in the noisy waiting room she was finally called back into a curtained off exam cubicle.

"Well, my dear, the rabbit died," the nurse said, smiling.

"What? What do you mean? What's a rabbit got to do with anything?" Elle was confused. Why was this woman talking about rabbits for God's sake?

"Oh, honey, it's just an expression. They use rabbits for the pregnancy test is all. Congratulations, you are definitely in a family way. You need to start taking your pre-natal vitamins, which the clerk at the desk will give you, and make an appointment right away with your family doctor back home."

"Uh, okay, sure," Elle said, gathering her purse and rushing out of the clinic into the bright spring sunshine.

Graduation was in three weeks and she was Valedictorian of her class. She had a speech to make and could not look pregnant in front of her whole class. She was hoping her mother and brother would come; they had said they'd try, but her dad was too sick now to travel.

She decided to just not eat for three weeks, or at least eat as little as possible, and decide what to do after graduation. She would have the summer to figure it out and to earn some money before entering the University of Georgia in Athens in September.

Between bouts of morning sickness which she had to hide from her roommate, studying for final exams, and worrying about the thing growing like a cancerous tumor inside her, the three weeks flew by. The vomiting and a diet of saltine crackers and sweet iced tea worked; Elle actually lost two pounds and although a bit more pale than usual, she looked stunning in her royal blue cap and gown.

She gave a moving speech about living the American dream, and told the graduates that she was living proof that if one worked hard and kept their eye on the ball, anyone could achieve their goals.

"I come from a background of poverty," she said proudly, "a poor girl of mixed heritage. But with the help and kindness of others I am going to college and will become a strong advocate for others. Use the talents you have been given, work hard, don't take no for an answer, and you will succeed!"

She held her diploma high above her head and the crowd cheered. Of course, what she didn't tell them was that a willingness to do whatever it took was also now a part of her philosophy, including using her physical assets to whatever degree was necessary.

No one from her family attended her graduation. Her mother had sent a Hallmark card congratulating her but she had signed it with her name instead of 'mother'. Thomas had called and said a few words; he had gotten a job in the mine and was going to follow in their father's footsteps, eking out a living below ground. He explained to her that they had new safety measures in place now; they wore masks so he wouldn't get the black lung disease and they had even raised the pay scale. He seemed happy and Elle supposed that was what mattered. He had met a girl and they would probably marry at Christmas time. She considered briefly asking him what a girl could do to get rid of a baby but decided against it. He would tell Joo-Eun and Elle didn't want to give her mother the satisfaction of saying that she had become a tramp.

The Moores were there of course; they presented her with a lovely diamond encrusted watch and took her to lunch at an old Southern mansion that had been converted into a restaurant. The food was served family style; bowls and platters of ham, fried chicken, collard greens with fatback, and mashed potatoes were placed on the table and diners helped themselves to as much as they wanted. Sugary sweet iced tea, cornbread muffins and buttered biscuits were served along with homemade jams and creamery butter.

They offered to let her remain living in their home through college and even help her buy a car for the commute, but Elle had decided that she would live on campus in a dorm; her scholarship and a Pell Grant would cover all the costs. All she had to do was earn money for her extra living expenses, clothes and so forth, but she was hoping to earn enough for an apartment eventually. She had no idea how she would earn the money, but she knew her secret power would be her best asset. She believed she was literally sitting on a fortune.

Rita looked relieved, Ted looked stricken, and Elle was subdued, even though she ate voraciously. She was starving and the crispy fried chicken, butter beans and potato salad quickly disappeared from her plate. When her skirt felt tight, she reached under her blouse and unbuttoned it, then refilled her plate.

"My, my child, you act like a starvin' refugee," Rita said, watching her eat with unaccustomed gusto.

"Just hungry, Aunt Rita. I've been too busy studying to eat. Now that exams are over, I'm making up for lost time." She smiled and buttered another biscuit.

"Well, if you two will excuse me for a minute, I'm gonna run to the powder room and pay the check," Rita said, blotting her lips with her napkin and pushing herself back from the table. Elle was not certain if it was an accident or done purposefully, but Rita had flashed Elle with a shot of her sparse graying bush as she stood.

Ahhh, she's not wearing underwear any more thought Elle. *Sensing competition perhaps? Well, she can have him!*

As soon as Rita had stepped out of hearing range, Elle turned to Ted. "Listen, I'm pregnant," she whispered. "What am I supposed to do? Got any suggestions?"

"Why are you asking me?" he whispered back at her. "Whose kid is it?"

"It's yours of course and you know it. You're the only one fucking me and you've been doing it since I was sixteen. And you better help me do something or I'm going to have a nice long talk with Auntie Rita and we'll see what she thinks about it. Maybe she'll want to adopt your baby."

"She won't believe you. But I'll help you anyway, because I'm a nice guy. Daddy is gonna miss that sweet pussy of yours too. Maybe I'll come and visit you sometimes in Athens." He took a sip of his coffee, he continued, "call my office tomorrow and I'll give you the name of a doctor who will take care of everything. Now shut up about it."

He smiled as they watched Rita return to the table putting her credit card back into her purse.

"The bill is paid and I'm ready to go if you two are."

"Sure thing, darlin'," Ted said, leaning over to kiss his wife's cheek.

As they headed to the car, and during the long ride home, Ted sat in the back seat and never took his eyes off of Elle. She could feel his eyes burning into the back of her head and couldn't decide what to make of it. Was he angry? Sad about the thought of losing his unborn child? She finally decided that it was a look of sincere concern. He was just worried about her. Right? She hoped that was the answer, because she had never felt more alone in her life. Why did everyone end up using her and then tossing her aside? She renewed her vow to begin being the one who used.

She was so full of fried chicken and biscuits she felt like throwing up, and the lump in her throat threatened to choke her. The Moores had given her a place to live and been kind to her in many ways, but they had also destroyed a part of her, a kernel of innocence, now shriveled and black, that could never be regrown.

As instructed, Elle called Ted Moore's office and he gave her the name of a clinic on the southeastern fringes of Rome, which he told her catered to students in just her predicament. Everything could be handled anonymously.

"Will you come with me?" she asked, suddenly afraid of going alone.

"Absolutely not. I wish I could, believe me, but it's just not possible. Too many people in this town know my face. I took a big chance just paying for this." His voice dropped to a whisper. "Listen, Daddy loves his baby girl. Doesn't he show you how much he loves you? But he can't risk getting caught by Mommy. That would ruin everything. Don't worry, you'll be just fine. Daddy will always take care of you."

Two days later she showed up alone, on time for her appointment, and scared to death. Her hands were shaking and she felt light headed. There was no one, not a soul on earth, whom she could ask to accompany her. Ted

Moore was the only logical candidate and he had flatly refused again. She would have to rely on herself from now on, she knew. She had been stupid not to make him put on one of those rubbers they talked about in health classes, but she was too embarrassed to bring it up. He was the man; she figured he should know what he was doing. Big mistake. The only thing he was concerned about was having an orgasm inside 'his baby', not anything that might grow into one as a result.

She hated this thing growing inside her and couldn't wait to get it out. What if it looked like him? What if it liked to fuck little girls like he did? Gross.

"Miss Smith?" the nurse asked, standing at the swinging door with a clipboard.

"Jane Smith, yes ma'am," replied Elle.

"Come on back. Mister Smith has sent us over a money order to pay in full for the service. We're ready for you now."

Elle followed the nurse back into a treatment room with a hospital type bed, an intravenous set up, and lots of other shiny instruments she had never seen before.

At least it looks clean, she thought.

"Take off all your clothes, dear, and put this gown on, open in the back. Then lie down on the bed and put your feet in these stirrups," the nurse explained. "We'll be with you in a minute. Is anyone coming to be with you? The father perhaps?"

"No. No one."

"All right then. You can just stay here and sleep after the procedure until you feel up to leaving by yourself."

Elle did as she was told, shivering from a mixture of fear and the icy cold temperature of the room. It was humiliating to be here all alone. Obviously other girls had someone to come with them, help them get home, and make sure they were all right.

Well, fuck it. I'll take care of myself. Gotta get used to that. It's just me and my pussy now, against the world. And we're gonna do just fine.

Just when she thought she couldn't stand the cold any longer, the nurse returned with a man whom Elle assumed was the doctor. He didn't introduce himself, just told her to scoot her hips down to the end of the table, relax her knees, and take a deep breath.

He put his gloved hands on her knees, forcing them apart.

"This is going to feel cold and you may feel a pinch or two, but it's not going to hurt," the nurse said, as the doctor sat down on a stool, rolled himself over between her legs, and snapped on a huge silver light.

The warmth from the light felt good to Elle, and just as she began to relax, she felt him push some kind of metal instrument deep inside her and she did feel the pinch. She hoped he was pinching the thing growing inside her, killing it.

"Push," the doctor told her. Then, "Good, now push again. And again. Okay good. You can relax now."

She felt a warm gushiness between her legs and some cramping, like when she had a bad period.

"Is it gone? Is the thing gone?" she asked softly.

"If you are referring to the fetus, yes, it is no longer there. You are not pregnant now. You can push yourself back up on the table and relax. Nurse, get her a blanket please. She's shivering."

The doctor stripped off the rubber gloves, tossed them in the trash, and walked out carrying a silver bowl filled with blood and a tiny male fetus that, had it been allowed to grow, would indeed have been the spitting image of Ted Moore and been similarly endowed.

Elle had no idea how long she had slept, but when she opened her eyes the room was dark and quiet. It took her a few moments to realize where she was. She was alone and when she moved her legs she felt sore and stiff. She also realized that she had towels packed between her legs.

She was momentarily horrified that they had somehow damaged her power dome - her ticket to a successful future. Then she remembered why she was here and what had taken place.

"It's gone," she whispered to herself. "It's gone and I am free now. College and law school, here I come!"

She moved her legs to the side of the stainless steel bed and tried to sit up, but was intensely dizzy and lay back down. She also realized she was thirsty as all hell; her mouth felt like it had been packed with cotton balls.

"Nurse," she managed to croak. "Nurse!"

A young black woman opened the door and said, "Yes, miss? Nurse is done gone but I here to help."

"Can I get some water please?"

The girl closed the door and returned quickly with a plastic cup filled with warm tap water. Elle drank it gratefully through the bent straw, propping herself up on one elbow.

"I feel very dizzy," she told the girl. "Is that normal? Am I okay?"

"Yes, miss, you okay. That's normal. I done had three abortions myself and you can see I'm okay. You jest rest a little while longer and you be fine."

Elle dozed back off, huddling under the thin woolen blanket, and when she woke again she immediately knew that she felt better. She sat up, dropped her legs over the side of the bed, and stood without any dizziness. The towels between her legs were awkward, but she waddled over to the chair where her clothes were and began dressing.

"Not so fast, miss," said the aide coming back into the room. "Lay back down so I can take a look, make sure you not bleedin'"

Elle did as she was told; she lay back down, propped her feet back in the stirrups, and allowed the young girl to remove the towels and perform a cursory examination.

"Are you a nurse?" she asked.

"No, jest a Certified Nurses Aid. Took a class at the junior college. But I can tell if there's a problem and if they is I'll call the real nurse."

Elle could not see the girl's head but felt her fingers probing and heard her 'ooohing and aaaahing' from time to time.

"You gots one fine looking pussy, miss," she said, washing her with cold cloths. "Very pretty. Kinda shaped like a heart. No bleedin' though and everything look good."

"Well, gee, thanks. Can I go now?" Elle was anxious to put this whole episode behind her. Cold and aching, she desperately wanted a long hot shower.

The girl stood up smiling. "Yeah, you can go, but you ever want to do it with a girl, you give me a call. I eat you out good and proper, miss, like you never had before from no man." She wiggled her tongue for emphasis.

Relieved to know that she still had her power, even with a female, she said, "Yes, I'll be sure to call. Do I need to take any medications or anything?"

"No, jes take it easy for a few days. No sex for six weeks. And if you don't want this to happen again, get you some birth control. Better yet, stay away from mens and let me take care of you." She winked and smiled, showing yellowed and gapped teeth.

"Thanks for the offer," Elle said. "But I've got plans that don't include you."

The girl looked disappointed but smiled again and left Elle alone to wipe herself up and finish dressing.

Surprisingly, the girl's crude come-on had served to buoy Elle's spirits. She had made a mistake getting pregnant and would never let that happen again.

What she could not know was that the doctor had severed her fallopian tubes and she would never be able to have children, even when much later in life she would want to. He fervently believed that women who killed their unborn children should never be allowed to have an opportunity to kill another one. The 'spaying' as he thought of it was his moral justification for performing the abortions, which were very profitable in a college town. He further justified his actions by telling himself that if he didn't perform them, the girls would harm themselves in an effort to get rid of the unwanted pregnancies. He was doing God's work and surely God would not begrudge him a small profit for his efforts on His behalf.

Chapter 11

Georgia Bulldogs and Things That Byte

One chilly fall Saturday, just as Elle was getting settled into her University of Georgia dorm room - thankfully a single this time - a package arrived for her. The knock at the door startled her out of a reverie - she had been staring out of the third floor window at a beautiful stand of Georgia pine trees interlaced with bare branched dogwood trees. A few trees were showing brilliant fall colors; just enough to bring on a rare mood of homesickness for the always brilliant foliage in the hills of Virginia this time of year.

Halloween was a holiday that all children - rich and poor - could enjoy and this was one part of her childhood that she could remember fondly. It hadn't cost much to create a costume made of sheets, old grown up's clothes, or Papier-mâché masks. Pumpkins and candles were purchased for mere pennies at the five and dime store, and piles of leaves to jump into were free for the raking.

After signing for the package, she ripped it open to find a small black velvet box and a note from her mother.

Dear Elle,

Sorry to tell you that your dad has pass away; he out of pain now and with our Heavenly Father. Your father good man, even though he not always act so good. He loved you very much.

This gift is way of saying I love you too and hope you have very happy life. I was going to give it to you on your 16th birthday but you already gone by then.

Come home some time and see Thomas and me. He marry now and got baby girl. His wife a pig and not good housekeeper but he love her so I guess okay.

You be good girl. Love, Your momma, Joo-Eun

Elle tossed the note aside and opened the box. She decided she would delay thinking about her father and be sad later. Her feelings about him were a jumble of mixed emotions, including love, hate, and passion. She just didn't feel like dealing with all those emotions at the moment.

Inside was a small jade cabochon surrounded by tiny diamonds and emeralds. It was delicate and lovely; not nearly so costly as the pieces of jewelry given to her by Ted Moore, but much more special because it had belonged to her mother. She had seen her wear it many times, always explaining that it had belonged to her mother and her grandmother before her.

Elle was very touched that her mother was passing down this family heirloom to her; after all, she could have given it to Tommy's wife or saved it for her granddaughter.

She cried as she placed it around her neck and fastened the clasp. This gift was much more than a mere piece of jewelry. It tied her to her family, her ancestry, and gave her a feeling of belonging. Now she not only had a future, she had a past as well. One day she would pass this necklace down to her own daughter, perhaps on her sixteenth birthday.

Glancing in the mirror from the necklace down to the new and still freshly reddened tattoo above her left breast, she felt complete, and filled with hope for a bright future.

The tattoo had been an inspiration and was her flag of independence. She had done it on the spur of the moment one day when she was shopping and walked past a tattoo parlor near the campus bookstore. With her newly adopted motto of pussy power, she was nobody's blindly-led baby any more. Her father was gone, Ted Moore was finally out of her life and out of her womb, and from now on she would control her own destiny.

Elle loved the sprawling campus of the University of Georgia and very quickly adopted the Georgia Bulldog mascot as her own. Her dorm room was filled with pennants, posters and a large stuffed dog. She planned, as time would allow, to attend every football game 'between the hedges'. College was exciting; a whole new world even brighter than Darlington, with students from all over the world. She was no longer an oddity or an outsider.

Ted Moore had offered to put her up in an apartment and give her an allowance in exchange for access to her body, but she had chosen to make a clean break of those ties. Rita had looked relieved when she had moved out of Suzanne's room, even though Elle was sure she would miss their shopping trips and gossip sessions. He had persisted but when she threatened to tell Rita, he finally stopped calling.

Without his support, she knew she needed to find a job, so she turned to the Yellow Pages. It was important to find something that paid well and yet allowed her to work only evenings and weekends, leaving her free for a full load of classes. Maybe even one where she could study when things were slow. Waitressing perhaps?

Thumbing through the thick book she spotted a category called 'Escort Services'. *Hmmmm*, she thought, *I could be an escort. How hard is that? Some man needs a date for an event, I get all dressed up and walk in on his arm. His friends are impressed. Easy as pie.*

She called several services to determine whether or not they had openings and how much they paid.

Bull Dog Escorts seemed like the best bet, and she loved their tag line: The best darned dates between the hedges. They also said they paid the most, so she made an appointment to apply.

They took her picture, had her fill out an application, and asked her if she'd had a medical check up lately.

"Yes, but why do you need to know about my health?" she asked.

"Well, sometimes our clients like to receive *extra services* if you know what I mean, and we like our escorts to be clean and healthy. No diseases. That's bad for business."

Elle got the idea quickly; escort meant much more than merely accompanying someone.

"Do these *extra services* pay *extra* money?" Elle asked.

"Of course. You negotiate that on your own based on the client's needs, but we get a ten percent kick back. And don't think you can cheat us. Our clients are very loyal and we'll find out if you stiff us. No pun intended."

"No problem. I don't mind sharing. It's only fair," Elle replied. "When can I get my first job?"

"Soon, my dear. Very soon. I'm sure as soon as your picture gets posted in our catalog you will be very popular. We'll call you as soon as we get a request for your services."

Elle left feeling very hopeful. With their standard hourly rate plus those extra services the man had mentioned, she felt certain she could earn some serious money. She didn't need a lot, but money was a way of keeping score. The more she made, the more she was worth.

"Thanks for the good genes, Mom," she said, fingering the jade pendant.

Four days passed without a word, then the dorm phone rang and Elle had her first date. A retired cop named Stu Butler wanted her to escort him to dinner. It was his birthday and he was treating himself to a special night on the town. He had decided to look through the catalog and find someone fresh and new for the occasion. Elle's picture stood out like a flower in a mud pit, he told the manager.

His sixtieth birthday turned out to be very special indeed; the beginning of a new, sexually satisfying relationship that would turn into much, much more.

Retirement didn't suit him; his marriage to childhood sweetheart Judy was hanging on by a hair and his being home all day hadn't helped.

"If I'd have known you were such a bitch," he told his wife during one particularly loud argument, "I never would have retired."

"If I'd have known," she replied, "that you were such a pig I'd have killed you in your fuckin' sleep."

They actually cared deeply about each other but a cop's life is one of odd hours, days of being gone on stake outs, and rarely being home for any length of time. The phone would ring and he'd be strapping on his gun and out the door with barely a finger wave goodbye. Now he was underfoot twenty-four hours a day and she wasn't used to it. He also had developed some kind of new (at least she thought it was new) passion for sex that just plain annoyed her. Once or twice a month was more than enough as far as she was concerned. Beyond that was just unchristian and nasty.

Judy had taken to keeping a Bible and a rosary on her nightstand, reading passages aloud at bedtime, and hoping the presence of the Lord's word would dissuade Stu from groping at her or poking her in the back trying to play hide the weenie.

So now Stu devoted most of his days to buying guns, firing them on his favorite outdoor range, and studying all the new gadgetry available for electronic surveillance. He decided to get his private investigators license and hire out for security.

He passed out some cards among his fellow law enforcement contacts - Sandy Springs cops, Atlanta PD, GBI, and even a few feds he knew - and soon he had his first customer - me, the infamous Buckhead Madame. I requested a meeting with him in my Buckhead mansion.

"How did you get my number?" Stu asked, after being shown into my lavish, professionally decorated office. I thought my mansion was quite beautiful but Stu said he thought there was enough chintz, frills, Roman statuary, mirrors, and other crap in that house to make a queer throw up. Well, fuck, each to his own.

"We may have some law enforcement customers from time to time," I told him with a wink. "One of them gave me your card and suggested I call if I was serious about upgrading my security."

I gave Stu a tour of the mansion, finishing up in a hidden sub-basement that only me and the builder knew about. I suggested Stu make that room his electronics center for his monitors and taping equipment and only the two of us would have a key to the reinforced metal door. He readily agreed, gave me a price that he figured I would balk at but didn't, and we shook hands on the deal.

It took him a month to get the rooms wired, hidden cameras in place, and monitoring stations set up in what we came to call Room 69, but it eventually got done. It took longer than it should have because I wouldn't allow him to hire extra help, and he had to work in the girls' rooms when they were off duty or didn't have a customer, which was rare.

During the testing phases he watched so much sex action that he maintained a perpetual hard on and Elle had to work overtime keeping him satisfied. He poked at Judy as often as she would allow but that wasn't nearly enough. She thought he had lost his mind, especially when he tried new positions he had seen the girls perform.

They were a true odd couple - his nightstand with the golden tiger striped Desert Eagle and hers with the Holy Bible.

He was thrilled one night when he noticed that on her nightstand sat the blue bottle of exotic warming gel that I had given him as a little gift. He thought she had thrown it away, but there it was, sitting tantalizingly next to her pearl Crucifix.

"Oh, Mama," he murmured into her ear, reaching for the bottle. "Come to Papa." And boy, did she ever come. To Papa.

Chapter 12

Roxy's Doctor Feel Good

I had a very special man in my life. In spite of the fact that I was a madam and ran a sophisticated brothel, I needed the security and comfort that only a one on one, personal relationship could provide. Go ahead and call me silly but I just need a steady man.

I met and fell hard for the very handsome, muscular, and hairy-chested Dr. Garrett Poindexter, eminent Atlanta cosmetic surgeon, when I went to him for 'a little tune up'. His ads in the *Atlanta Constitution* caught my eye.

"Beauty really is only skin deep" the ads proclaimed. Another one read "You can judge a book by the cover - readers do it every day". Nothing like telling the truth I always say. He was just telling it like it is.

Over a period of years - we were together for a total of six blissful and Botox filled years - I ended up availing myself of his full menu of services, including a vaginal tightening, and he ended up availing himself of my full menu of services, including vaginal, oral and anal penetrating. It was, shall we say, a mutually beneficial relationship. We both got what we wanted. Well almost.

He wanted to dump his stupid simple-minded redneck wife (his words, not mine) and marry me and take me away from 'all this'.

"Are you crazy, Garrett?" I asked him. "Take me away from millions of dollars, a business I love, a gorgeous mansion, loyal customers, and every luxury a girl could ask for?" I didn't mention my little sessions now and then with Noir, or my secret obsession with Jade's pussy, because as a man he just wouldn't have understood. Men, especially macho men such as those attracted to surgery and other God-like professions, think their peckers are the be all and end all of sexual satisfaction. So talking about Noir and Jade would have made him crazy jealous. It didn't bother him that I still handled a few male clients, but lesbian interludes would not have flown. He is the only man I've ever known that was not turned on by girl on girl sex. If it didn't involve his own pecker, he just didn't get into it.

His argument was that my business would one day become a burden, or some crazy customer was going to shoot me, or some jealous wife was going to burn the house down, or some Baptist preacher was going to start a campaign to shut me down.

Well, every business has its problems but the call girl business is what I know and I wasn't worried. Jade was helping me keep the books straight. Stu Butler had a kick-ass security system set up and I had secret tapes on everyone that I hoped would bail me out in the event shit rained down on me, and money was pouring in. I was driving an alabaster white Mercedes-Benz SL500 convertible and had a tiny white miniature poodle named Cooter that sat at my feet and licked my toes adoringly.

Yeah, I told Garrett he would just have to take what I was willing to give. My life was just too damn good to trade it in for fidelity and the humdrum life of marriage. One man in my life? No women? No Noir and her mystical magical tongue? No Jade and her beautiful pussy and tantalizing tattooed tit? No fucking way.

But I wasn't stupid. I knew bad things could happen, and I made sure I had a solid Will & Testament locked in my desk drawer to take care of the people I care about. I was well aware of the fact that my businesses would not survive long without me, because I'm the driving force. I know what men like and what they will pay for. Sometimes, though, they surprise even me.

Chapter 13

Bye Bye Bulldogs, Hello Hot'lanta!

Four years attending the University of Georgia studying pre-law with a minor in international business and a second minor in Asian studies seemed to fly by for Elle, like a video tape in fast-forward mode.

There were times when she wasn't sure what day it was, and days blended seamlessly into nights. She rarely had a moment to reflect on her childhood back in Virginia; on those rare occasions when a memory would pop up unbidden from her subconscious, it almost seemed like those things had happened to another person.

Could she really have been a gangly, unkempt, clumsy girl who had been so desperate for love that she had screwed her own father? Had she really spent all those hours riding on dirty Greyhound Buses and tolerated the forced attentions of Ted Moore?

It seemed impossible. When she looked in the mirror now - and there was one above her bed at *Hot'lanta Belles* so she did that often - she saw a beautiful, sophisticated woman. One who was coifed, manicured, pedicured and twinkling with expensive jewelry on her fingers, toes, ankles, ears, belly button and labia.

Her life was full - she lived by a Daytimer - with classes, studying, dates with Stu (who she continued to see on a regular basis), clients at the mansion, and helping me manage my complicated duplicitous accounting system. Not to mention the occasional sessions that I demanded when I got into one of my 'pussy moods' as I called 'em.

She had warned me repeatedly that I should run my business in a more legitimate way, but I always replied, "Run a whore house accordingly to the law?" I mean, come on, that made no sense.

Elle finally relented and agreed that I had a point - the entire business was illegal so why keep honest books, but as anybody who has studied crime knows, it's the money that gets you in trouble. Especially since the inception of the Rico Act, where any assets obtained through illegal activities could be seized. And then she reminded me about the whole I.R.S. nightmare that has brought so many famous people to their knees.

"Honey, I've made a good living on my knees, so the damned I.R.S. don't scare me," was always my answer. Elle probably figured that I was counting on my many law enforcement clients to protect me, but Elle warned me more than once that if push came to shove they wouldn't stick their necks out for little old me.

And then one day Elle looked at her Daytimer and realized that she was about to graduate. It was May and final exams were over. She had been accepted to law school at prestigious Emory University, and her life was on track to be everything she had dreamed of on those long bus rides.

She invited her brother Tommy and her mother to attend, but she knew they wouldn't come because Georgia was a world away from their Virginia lives. She was a stranger to them and had never even met Tommy's two children - a boy and a girl - but he had at least sent her a Christmas card each year with their pictures. The kids were cute; she hoped that one day maybe she would have some that looked as adorable as her niece and nephew. They both had black hair and tiny upturned noses, but hazel eyes that reflected their American heritage.

Graduation was held in the University of Georgia's Ramsey Center and Elle was once again envious of all the joyous families gathered, congratulating her classmates, cheering as diplomas were handed out. These were the times when she wished that she had placed more value on family than on achievements, but those feelings usually only lasted a few moments, then she would realize that if she had stayed with her family she would probably be pregnant and working in a factory.

No, she'd rather have her life with its bright future and certain riches; a city life now that she was moving to Atlanta instead of commuting to *Hot'lanta Belles* from Athens several times a week.

She was looking forward to moving into a poolside garage apartment in the elite community of Morningside, which was conveniently near Emory's sprawling campus. The apartment was a deal she couldn't pass up; the Brookings family owned an international publishing company and would be in Europe for a year. They had offered her free room and board and in return she would keep an eye on the large mid-century style home, making sure the pool and grounds were maintained and the security system stayed armed.

Her little studio apartment had been built as a guest house and had beautiful French doors that opened onto the Spanish tiled pool deck. A housekeeper came twice a week to dust and water the plants and then there was a pool cleaner and lawn maintenance crews. None of them ever bothered her and she enjoyed the luxury of quiet and spaciousness the home offered for both entertaining and studying.

Living close to school would also allow her more time to take clients at the mansion, and more money to put into her growing bank account.

She'd found out that Noir was no longer working at *Hot'lanta Belles*; apparently she had been lured away for a life of luxury with some Hip Hop star who didn't want her seeing other men. Or women. Atlanta is a city with many different cultural and ethnic communities, and the music industry was growing by leaps and bounds and gaining a lot of prominence on the Hip Hop scene.

Elle wondered how me and my business were going to deal with losing Noir. We had done a threesome one time together and Noir was something else in the sack. She was in fantastic shape and seemed tireless, never broke a sweat no matter how vigorous things got, and was the most flexible person either of us had ever seen. She could put her ankles behind her head, or do a backbend and grab her ankles. When she did that, Elle nearly went nuts with excitement - you could always tell when Elle was excited 'cause she would bounce up and down on her toes. Noir could also do a split and pick up a coin from the floor with her pussy muscles; a trick I had only seen once before in my life. Elle and me fought over who would get to suck it back out. Noir charged clients extra for that kind of stuff, but for the boss, it was all free. Elle often talked about one particular night of three-way sex that had involved drizzled chocolate, warm honey, whipped cream - all things women love. Combine pussy, champagne, and acrobatics, and we both seriously wondered if the thug du jour Noir had left *Hot'lanta Belles* for was appreciative of what he had.

-Chapter 14-

Noir Comes and Goes

Hot'lanta Belles had customers from all walks of life, as you might imagine. Those 'walks' included both the cream of the crop and the crap that got left behind in the field to rot. Sometimes those field leavings managed to survive, and they matured into rotten, nasty human beings with bellies full of pork rinds, beer and hatred.

One of my very first customers, someone who actually gave me money long ago to get me started, was a tall, skinny cotton farmer named Jimmy Ray Bullard. He owned about two hundred acres of land up in Hart County, northeast of Atlanta, and even though he was now wealthy, he was one such full grown piece of white trash. But, I gotta take the bad with the good, and Jimmy Ray's money was as green as the rest. And long before the cream of the crop thought my business was good enough for them, Jimmy Ray was there, cash in hand.

Jimmy Ray was, of course, a supreme KKK card carrying racist, despising anyone who was not white. The sermons he listened to religiously every Sunday about loving thy neighbor didn't make a damn bit of difference. Somehow niggers, in his world, didn't qualify as neighbors.

My blonde hair and blue eyes were what first drew him to me years ago. Deep down, though, I always sensed that he had a good heart and I used to service him personally, even traveling up to his farm when he couldn't get away during picking season. That was long ago, well after his wife had passed away from cancer, but way before I had established *Hot'lanta Belles* and all its current glory.

When I got too busy running the business to continue to service most of my clients, I explained things to them and allowed them to preview and select another escort of their choice. Jimmy Ray always picked a white girl, finally settling on his favorite, a shy petite teenager. Once when I suggested he try 'something different', he exploded in a venomous rage.

"I ain't gonna fuck no spic, nigger, or chink, so forget about it, Miss Roxy." He grabbed his crotch and continued, "Little Jimmy here don't go into no cunts of them filthy whores. I'm fine with sweet Charity. Now just leave me be."

So, he stayed with Charity, an Iowa runaway, barely sixteen, with freckles and reddish blonde hair. She seemed to suit Jimmy Ray 'cause she was pretty inexperienced and he liked feeling superior to her. He could intimidate her and act like king of the mountain; with the older, more experienced girls that shit wouldn't fly.

One day Charity came to me and said she didn't want to entertain Jimmy Ray any more.

"Why?" I asked her. "You know you have to do who ever you're assigned to, Charity. Besides, he seems to really like you."

"He's just dirty, Miss Roxy. Can't you put him with somebody else? He stinks."

"Well, I'll try again, honey. But if he refuses, you're stuck and you can just consider it part of the job. There are gonna be men and women you don't like, but that's just too fuckin' bad."

The next time Jimmy Ray came in and signed in with the receptionist, I took him aside and told him that Charity was busy and he would have to spend the evening with someone else. It helped that he hadn't made an appointment so he couldn't expect his chosen girl to be free that night.

"The only person I have available tonight is Noir," I told him. "She's French, from the island of Barbados actually, and she is very, very good." Before he could object, I continued, "Jimmy Ray, she can teach Little Jimmy some new tricks. She can do things with him you've never even dreamed of." I reached over and rubbed his crotch for emphasis, and could feel his immediate response to the warmth of my hand. "So, are you man enough to fuck her brains out, Jimmy Ray, or are you scared of a little dark skinned island girl?"

"I ain't scared of nobody, let alone no foreign pussy. You bring me to her and I'll show her a thing or two. Me and my big ole pecker, we might just teach her how white men fuck."

I was proud of myself. Barbados? Noir was a country street girl from Fayetteville. Now I was gonna pair up a black whore with a white racist who could never seem to find time to take a shower. Let the games begin.

Noir answered my call and came slowly down the stairs wearing only a very small white lace teddy, surprised to see me standing in the foyer with Jimmy Ray. She raised her eyebrows questioningly, but I could see that Jimmy Ray was focused on her body, clearly visible through the white lingerie. She paused at the foot of the stairs and draped one leg over the banister, giving him a full view of her crotch. She began squeezing and releasing her pussy muscles, tightening and releasing the fabric of her panties, and pretty soon everyone was watching.

"Noir," I said, "this is Jimmy Ray. He would like to spend some time with you tonight. He's an old friend of mine and I'd appreciate it if you'd take especially good care of him."

Everybody in the house knew that Jimmy Ray was a racist; his bigoted rants had been heard many times, so Noir was very surprised that he had agreed to a session with her. She was a pro, however, and handled this job like any other.

She lifted her leg from the banister, stepped down, and held her hand out gracefully to Jimmy Ray. "Come with me, Jimmy Ray," she said, "and you will enjoy a night to remember."

Surprisingly, he took her hand and followed her meekly up the stairs, disappearing on the second floor landing, probably picturing her pussy muscles squeezing on his pecker. I heard her door click shut and waited at the foot of the stairs, expecting to hear her scream for help. When no further sounds were heard, I ran down to my video monitoring station to watch the session unfold. I was both curious and fearful for Noir's safety. I certainly didn't want her to be damaged, as that would not only be bad for business, it would be bad for my sex life as well.

I watched as Noir gently and patiently peeled Jimmy Ray's clothes off, piling them up at the foot of her canopied bed. First came the dusty cowboy boots, then the plaid western style shirt with the pack of cigarettes and lighter in the pocket. Then the worn out belt came off, followed by a pair of mud caked jeans.

As each piece of clothing came off, she made sure her fingers trailed down his thin body, and I noticed that he had his eyes closed. Finally, she pulled down his once white Hanes briefs, turning them inside out. Her nose turned up when she saw the brown stains that smeared the entire backside of the briefs.

She stood, took his hand, and led him toward her bathroom. I heard the shower come on and they disappeared into a cloud of steam. Stu had placed a camera in the bathroom, but the lens was not immune to steam. I made a mental note to speak to him about that.

I waited patiently, sipping hot tea that I made for myself, and finally they emerged from the bathroom, Jimmy Ray now sparkling clean and smiling bigger than the jackass he was. It looked to me like he had lost a good deal of weight. Was he just working hard or was something wrong with him?

Noir laid down on the bed, spreading her legs wide open, and motioning Jimmy Ray to join her. By now Little Jimmy was at full attention. It was apparently not nearly as racist as its master, because it sought Noir like a heat seeking missile. Realizing that she didn't need to do any acrobatics to satisfy him, she locked her ankles around his waist and allowed him to dominate her, even cooing "Yes, Master" to him, as he pumped away. It was over quickly.

Satisfied, he rolled off of Noir and said, "Now, that's how us white men do it, girlie. Whaddya think of that, huh?"

"Oh, it's the best fuck I've ever had, Master. Can we do it again?"

"Nah, not tonight. You done got all you're gonna git outa me for one night."

He stood and began getting dressed, so I went back up to the foyer and awaited his departure.

Jimmy Ray came down the stairs smiling, his racist heart beating a new tune.

"Did you enjoy your evening, Jimmy Ray?"

"Yes, Miss Roxy, I did. But you won't be seeing no more of me. I can't take no more little blue pills. Doc says they're bad for my heart. I reckon I'll just have to take care of Little Jimmy myself and work my farm for the time I got left."

He kissed me sadly on the cheek and walked out the door, humming *Dixie*. It was the last time I ever saw him.

If anything, the evening with Jimmy Ray raised Noir's standing in my eyes even higher. She had been brave and smart all at once. I didn't know what I would do without her, but one day I was forced to face that possibility.

Another one of Noir's steady clients was an up and coming Hip Hop music producer and recording artist, who called himself Fabulous Cash Money. 'Fabulous' for short. His real name was Fabian Coleman and he was the president of *Durty South Records*. His newest venture was a line of phat hip hop clothing he was calling *Durty Rags*.

The whole Atlanta Hip Hop scene was blinking and flashing like strobe lights in a 70's disco, and Fabulous had just enough good looks and music talent to get him from being a dime a dozen party dee jay to the big time.

I asked him one time why he came to my mansion for sex, since I was sure he was surrounded by willing groupies and hangers-on. He explained that he preferred to handle his business on a professional level and not have to deal with the drama, tears, broken hearts, and bitch fights that would break out when he chose one girl over another. It was just cleaner and easier to come to the mansion, get laid in royal fashion with Noir, and leave, hassle free.

"I don't want to worry about catchin' something, or some bitch turnin' up pregnant either," he said. "Man such as myself got to be careful, yo."

Of course that was before he fell head over high heeled patent leather boots in love with Noir and her trick pussy.

I saw it coming and tried to steer him to other girls, but he was dead set on having Noir and none other. I even offered to do him myself, and he turned me down. First time that had ever happened to me and I have to say I was a bit miffed. I think Fabulous was as much of a racist as old Jimmy Ray was, just the other side of the k..k..koin.

Looking back, I wish I would have tried harder but I'm not sure anything would have kept Noir from being attracted to the Hip Hop lifestyle - the flash, the cash, the bling, and the sting of being around the head bee himself.

For six months, Fabian, a/k/a Fabulous, paid Noir visits, each time staying longer and each time with more of an entourage in tow than the time before. It got so that his entire posse would pull into the circular drive - including his personal diamond black Bentley GT Continental. The driveway and portico would be lined with Range Rovers and Cadillac Escalades, sound systems thumping behind windows I knew were tinted way too dark to be legal, and either frightening or intimidating my other clientele.

I knew I had to do something, but I didn't want to offend either Noir or Fabulous. Before I could talk to Elle or Stu, however, my dilemma was solved. Noir quit.

It happened rather quickly and unexpectedly one evening, when Fabulous made a dramatic entry into the mansion's foyer, a white fur coat draped over his shoulders and his jewelry flashing underneath the huge Austrian crystal chandelier. I damn near had to put sunglasses on.

Before the receptionist could call Noir and let her know that her 'man' had arrived, she came down the stairs carrying a suitcase and a hanging bag.

"That all you got, baby girl?" Fabulous asked.

"A course not, Fab. Somebody need to go up and git the rest of my stuff."

Fabulous snapped his fingers and one of his body guards headed up the stairs, a bulge visible beneath his sharkskin suit jacket.

"Noir," I said, stepping toward them. "What's going on?" Where are you going with that luggage?"

"I'm sorry, Roxy, I was gonna talk to you, really. My man Fabulous here," she said, reaching up to stroke his cheek, "he want me to come and live with him. He don't want me doin' no other men 'cept him. So, much as I appreciate all you done for me, I am gonna go and be with him. Ain't that right, Boo?"

She tried to hug me but I was much too angry for that nonsense. How dare this woman - this street whore that I brought in to my business and taught her everything she knows - how dare she just walk out on me like this. I felt betrayed and hurt and about as mad as I've ever been in my life.

I pushed her away from me and slapped her across the face with every ounce of strength I could muster.

"Get out then, *Lashonda*, and when this thug gets tired of you, and he will, don't even think about coming back here. You are done. Finished. And I will make sure every other escort service in Atlanta knows what a treacherous no good bitch you are."

Noir raised her hand to slap me back, but Fabulous grabbed her arm and dragged her out the door. "Come on, Boo," he said. "Let's get outa here." Just before he reached the door he turned back to me and said, "Yo, don't you never touch my woman again, bitch. I'll bust a cap in your fat white ass, fo sho."

Soon the body guard came down stairs carrying four suitcases, two under each arm like they weighed nothing and followed them down the front steps.

The caravan pulled away and although I was still furious, I couldn't help but feel a bit sad at the loss of my employee, my lover, and one of my true success stories. In one rash decision, chasing what she thought was fame and fortune, Noir had once again become Lashonda Johnson, a project rat from the streets. Oh, she wouldn't realize it for a while, but that's just exactly what had happened. As far as getting shot by Fabulous or one of his thugs, I wasn't worried. Hell, I've been threatened by men much more dangerous than some two bit rapper in a fur coat. The men you have to fear are the ones who never say a word. The ones that don't make threats, just act.

Chapter 15

Noir Becomes A Durty Girl

*F*abian Coleman had hit the big time and was planning to ride the Hip Hop wave as far as it would take him. He had come up dirty, snot nosed and poor, one of three boys born to a single teenaged crack head mother, in a Grady Homes project apartment. From his rare excursions on MARTA, he caught occasional glimpses of Atlanta's gleaming sky scrapers and the wealth surrounding him, and he intended to get his share of the peach pie. After meeting the luscious Noir, he decided that he wanted her super fine ass next to him on the ride up. He had seen a lot of pussy in his time, but never one as exquisite as hers. He even wrote rap lyrics about her.

During his rapid rise to fame, he had purchased a fifteen acre compound, complete with its own music recording studio, in Union City, about thirty minutes south of downtown Atlanta. The offices of *Durty South Records* and *Durty Rags* were located in a penthouse suite in Buckhead at the corner of Lenox Road and Peachtree Street, conveniently quite near *Hot'lanta Belles*.

In addition to the compound and the penthouse office suite, he owned a high-rise condominium in TWELVE Condominiums in downtown Atlanta's Atlantic Station Development that he used strictly for out of town business guests and entertaining.

After becoming *Fabulous Cash Money*, first as a dee jay, then later as president of his own companies, he had enjoyed the company of many women. As a regular guest on BET television, he never lacked for offers of booty, both black and white. But after a short time, he tired of them and their spoiled, whining, self-centered behavior. It had gotten so bad that, following a tip from another record producer, he had started visiting *Hot'lanta Belles* so he could get laid and have a decent conversation at the same time. He could also just leave when he was ready and not have to worry about entanglements or female demands on his time.

Once he had begun seeing Noir, however, it had been a short trip from infatuation to fascination, and then a hard stop at full fledged adoration. She was not just a limber and creative performer in bed, she read the newspaper, she read books, and she kept up with fashion and music. A man could only fuck for so long, and after that he needed good company. After all, he couldn't confide or converse with any of the groupies and hangers on in his business, so he needed someone he could trust.

He had tested Noir, telling her things that no one else knew, and then waiting to see if word spread. It never had. Apparently working at *Hot'lanta Belles* had been a good training ground for her, but now it was time to pull her away so her body would be his exclusively. Along with adoration came a sense of proprietary ownership. She would be his and his alone.

He bought her a platinum silver supercharged V8 Range Rover that was a twin to his own, and gave her a black American Express card so that she could shop to her heart's content. He wanted her to look the part as his woman, his bitch, although he would never call her that to her face.

His newest business venture was *Durty Rags*, a line of Hip Hop clothing aimed at teens and young urbanites, and he liked to say that it was 'taking off like a drive by'. He hoped that showing up at media events, premiers, and concerts with Noir on his arm wearing some of the *Durty Rags* clothing would boost sales and gain him more recognition. *Damn, the woman look good in that shit*, he thought. But he had to admit she looked even better with nothing on.

He was crazy about her body and the seemingly impossible athletic feats she performed to his amazement. He fully recognized why Roxy had been so pissed off to lose her. Noir had told him how she was Roxy's favorite female fuck partner, but Noir had also said that she never really enjoyed that. She preferred men such as him with huge cocks and powerful tongues themselves that could pleasure her.

Within six months of Noir moving in with Fabulous, they were the toast of the Atlanta music business and were invited everywhere - the new media darlings could always be counted upon to strike a dramatic and beautiful picture on the red carpet or the dance floor.

One day Noir approached Fabulous with her own business idea, and as usual her timing was perfect.

They were making love on a white angora rug in front of the stone fireplace in his condo. Fabulous's ebony skin was glistening with sweat and his muscles were taut with the physical exertion and the tension of heightened passion.

Noir showed no signs of exertion; she fluidly twisted, turned and moved with grace from one position to another, sometimes on top of him and sometimes beneath him, but always moving, writhing and undulating.

"God, girl, you're killing me," he said. "Be still for a minute. Let a brother catch his fuckin' breath."

She merely laughed softly and bent to take him into her mouth again, causing him to groan and lift his hips toward her.

Before he could come, she bit him just enough to cause him to utter a 'yip', and then she sat on his face. As he began licking her, she spun around, bent over, and took him into her mouth again, never losing contact with his tongue. Her hips and his tongue moved rapidly up and down rhythmically, but again before he could come, she moved and took him inside her. He filled his mouth with a beautiful brown breast instead of her soft pink pussy, and at last she allowed him to climax. He shuddered violently and rolled over so that she was lying next to him. His smile was her reward, although she supposed she could also consider the new emerald cut diamond ring on her finger as a reward too.

When he could breathe normally again, he said, "Now, what was that business idea you had, Noir?"

"Well, I been thinkin' that a calendar would be a cool idea, twelve months with each month a picture of me in a different *Durty Rags* outfit. Whaddya think?"

"I think that's a *fabulous* idea," he said laughing and fondling her breast. "Matter of fact, I'll talk to the marketing company tomorrow and we'll get started on it soon. I want my girl to be seen but not touched!" He emphasized his ownership by squeezing her breast until she yelped and stood up.

"Stop it, man. You got no right to hurt me!"

"Yeah, hell I do, *Lashonda*," he said cruelly, "and don't you never forget it. I own you lock, stock, and pussy."

Noir didn't bother to argue with him, because deep down she knew he was right. What was she gonna do, go back to the street? She looked around at her elegant surroundings and decided that being owned by the world famous *Fabulous Cash Money* was not such a bad deal. Was it?

Chapter 16

Let's Make a Deal

Nine well dressed men sat somewhat stiffly and subdued around an ebony 18th century conference table, conversing about international news, the Atlanta Braves latest player scandal, and how stupid their wives were. Oh, they didn't use the word 'stupid', but that was the consensus. Wives had no idea what it took to be successful in the business world, no idea how hard they worked, and no appreciation for the sacrifices the men made every day. The least they could do was come across with a little enthusiastic sex now and then, but no, that seemed to be too much to ask.

When the door opened they all sat up a little straighter and all eyes turned toward Elle, as she strode to the head of table and dropped a thick sheaf of papers onto the glass top. When the papers hit the table it sounded like a gun shot. For some of them, it might as well have been. A warning shot across the bow - get this deal done or else.

She had dressed carefully for this meeting - her most serious 'I'm not fucking around' power suit. She had chosen a custom tailored pantsuit in a dove gray wool-flannel pinstripe, tortoise shell glasses strictly for effect, subdued make-up, and her hair was pulled up in a severe bun. For a simple touch of richness she had placed two pearl and silver geisha hair ornaments artfully woven through the center of the bun.

She wanted no one around this table to doubt that she meant business, and it seemed to be working. The men, all nine of them, were focused on her, watching her face. No eyes strayed downward to her breasts, no eyes

wandered around the room, and no one spoke.

"Good morning, gentlemen," she said pleasantly. "Are we ready to begin?"

Elle distributed copies of the documents she had brought in, giving each man a copy.

This deal was the culmination of her career. Every man and woman she had fucked, including her father and her surrogate father Ted Moore, every degrading sexual act she had performed for money, all the days and nights without sleep, seven years of college, and even her carefully choreographed marriage to Senator Harrison Whitmire, had come down to this day.

"Look the agreement over please. If you have any questions, speak up. Otherwise sign where my assistant has flagged, initial the bottom of each page, and pass your copy back to me. Let's get this done." To lighten the mood a bit she added, "I've got a hair appointment in thirty minutes."

Relieved chuckles punctuated the icy cold air of the conference room. Several of the men let out deep breaths and visibly relaxed. Maybe she wasn't such a dragon lady after all.

As she waited for their signatures, Elle tapped her long ivory lacquered nails against the table top, making a staccato sound in the otherwise quiet room. She sighed and made a show of looking at her watch.

"Gentlemen?"

There was actually no big hurry; she just wanted to create an atmosphere of urgency. She would allow no time for second thoughts or redundant questions. There would be no back tracking, no hesitancy, and definitely no balking.

Slowly, one bound set at a time, the documents were pushed back to her, fully executed. As the last one reached her hands, she stacked them up, shoved them back into their folder, and stood.

As if in response to some unseen and unheard signal, the conference room door opened and two butlers entered, white cloths draped formally over their arms. They were carrying trays of fluted glasses filled with bubbling champagne. Another butler followed carrying two silver trays of

chocolate dipped strawberries and several varieties of caviar canapés.

"Shall we toast to our mutually beneficial agreement?" Elle asked.

The nine men, including two Saudis, three Japanese, one German, one Londoner, and two Americans, stood, shook hands, and smiled for the first time since Elle had walked into the room. They spoke the common language of money, and each gratefully accepted a glass of Veuve Clicquot and formed an admiring circle around Elle.

She offered a toast, "To success at any cost," she said. "What we have accomplished today will rock the world of cellular communications for years to come. We have made history today, gentlemen, and you can all be proud." *Not to mention stinking goddamn rich* she thought.

Clinking glasses and murmurs of 'here, here' and 'chin chin' masked Elle's subtle departure. The deal was done and she was anxious to get home and get ready for the reception being held in her honor that evening.

It seemed to the men that her departure rendered the room dark, airless, and without life. After a few minutes of back slapping and self-congratulatory camaraderie, they drifted out of the room, secretly casting their eyes about for the alluring Elle Corday-Whitmire, Esquire. None of them were lucky enough to catch so much as a glimpse of her.

The ninety billion dollar deal, Elle's biggest since joining the firm, united three of the world's largest telecommunications companies into one super conglomerate that had secretive plans to monopolize international cellular services.

Elle had been hired for her abilities as a rain maker; men were so drawn to her that she was able to form relationships that resulted in complex deals requiring many billable law firm hours. She could keep them talking endlessly, unaware of the ticking time clock. By the time they got the bill, either the deal was done and they were happy, or they were so enamored of Elle and desperately hoping to get into her pants that they didn't care about the cost of time spent in her company.

Billable hours are the life blood of law firms and from the fifty dollar research assistants to the thousand dollar attorneys, time sheets were maintained with a scrupulous attention to detail that NASA would envy.

After graduating from the highly respected and top ranked law school at Emory University and passing her bar exams on the first try, a rare achievement, Elle decided some pay back was in order. She had been given many opportunities - from the McFarland Foundation to Roxy's *Hot'lanta Belles* - that were born of generosity. It was time she exhibited a little generosity of her own.

She was still living in the small poolside apartment because even after the homeowners returned from Europe they wanted her to stay, and her living expenses were minimal. So, Elle joined the staff of the Greater Atlanta Free Legal Clinic, which offered a wide range of legal services to homeless and indigent citizens. Landlord disputes, child custody issues, Social Security entanglements, disability insurance claims, and much more were tackled and litigated by the firm's twelve unpaid attorneys. Sometimes they lost, but more often than not, just based on sheer determination and a will to succeed, they were able to obtain satisfactory results for their clients.

The third case that landed on what Elle euphemistically called her 'desk' was that of a sixteen year old single mother, black, homeless, and without anything to her name except a grocery bag filled with baby stuff and a pocket full of WIC vouchers.

Cassondra Jenkins had initially come into the clinic to sit in the relative coolness and safety, to nurse her baby and use the bathroom. When no one ran her out, she ended up spending the entire day there and was still stretched out on two of the orange plastic chairs, her infant sleeping peacefully on her chest, when Elle began closing up for the day.

"Young lady," she said, "you're gonna have to leave now. Do you have somewhere to go?"

"No Ma'am," she answered, "but I'll git out 'cho way now." She began gathering up her things and strapping her tiny infant into a jury rigged contraption across her chest.

"Come back into my office," Elle told her. "Let's talk for a minute. You can't just take a baby out into the street with no place to go."

The girl followed Elle back into the darkened hallway and sat in the designated 'client' chair next to her so called desk.

Before Elle realized it, the baby, sucking on Cassondra's pinky finger, had fallen sound asleep again, and Cassondra had told Elle the story of how she had come to be homeless and a parent - two things no one should ever be.

Elle took notes on a yellow legal pad and soon decided that more than anything else, this girl needed someone to stand up for her. She had been strong enough to stand up for herself and make her own way, but Cassondra had been so beaten down my life's circumstances, she was so bereft of love, there was no room inside her for hope to grow.

Cassondra had not always been poor or homeless. Her father, however, had died in an auto accident - he had been hit by a Coca-Cola delivery truck - and his new wife had taken all the insurance money and moved back to her hometown in western Tennessee. She left Cassondra and her brother in the apartment with the rent paid for one month and they had what food was in the refrigerator and what change was in the cookie jar.

When the landlord threw them out after two months of non-payment of rent, they had each gone their separate ways, staying with friends, relatives, wherever they could crash for the night. The inevitable happened and one of the 'cousins' had gotten Cassondra pregnant, then refused to take any responsibility.

"I can help you, girl," Elle told her. "I will make Coca-Cola sorry their driver killed your daddy. But for now, you can stay here. We have a room in the back with a cot for when we have to work late. There's a refrigerator in the break room that's always filled with leftover pizza and Chinese take out. You'll see. Things are going to get a lot better for you real soon."

On Cassondra's behalf, Elle sued the good folks at Coca-Cola, who had denied any responsibility for the contracted driver or leased vehicle. After a few anonymous calls to the newspapers and local television stations, and several heart rending interviews that featured the adorable infant boy, Coca-Cola folded like a stack of laundry.

The headlines read:

HOMELESS TEEN WINS
MILLION DOLLAR SETTLEMENT
Coca-Cola ADMITS LIMITED LIABILITY

The clinic retained only filing fees and expenses, set up a trust account for Cassondra and her son, and made sure that she got the supervision she needed to take care of herself and her child.

Elle was interviewed on *Good Morning Atlanta* and Court TV. Ratings for both shows soared and she got a call from Carlyle, Kilpatrick, and Powell, LLP. Was she interested in joining their prestigious firm?

Yes, she most definitely was, and within three years she had manhandled and engineered the biggest telecommunications merger in history, and her name was being added to the masthead. She had also managed to marry and thoroughly pussy whip the state's most eligible bachelor, a man she needed but loved much less than he loved her.

Chapter 17

A Not So Cordial Invitation

One of my least favorite parts of the day has always been reading the mail. I rarely get love letters or birthday cards; I just run a service business that is focused on the customer and his or her needs. My personal life is of no consequence to anyone except myself and perhaps Garrett.

The mail was always bills, requests for charitable donations, and sometimes threatening letters from right wing Bible thumping lunatics or cheated-on wives who had somehow discovered their husband's infidelity. I usually handed those over to Stu, who either followed up on them in some way or tossed them into a drawer for further review.

So the day I received not one but two horrifying pieces of mail was a red letter day indeed.

The first was a form letter from the Internal Revenue Service, cordially inviting me to attend a full audit for the previous three years. The audit would be conducted in their Peachtree Street offices. The instructions said I should bring all receipts and documents supporting all entries on all returns, and that I should also bring all employee records, including social security numbers, addresses, and all banking records. I figured I was pretty much fucked. It wasn't bad enough that business was slow, I had lost Noir to the high life and Elle to the low life of lawyers, now I had to justify all my records to the fucking I.R.S.

I decided to toss that letter aside and open another one that was from

Garrett's medical offices. What was this, a bill? Was he billing me now for my Botox injections? No wonder he hasn't been returning my calls this week.

The letter, however, was not from Garrett. It was from his wife, on office stationery.

Dear whore,

Stay away from my husband. He has confessed all and has chosen to stay with me and to honor our marriage vows. He has explained to me how you tricked him and lured him into doing things that are against his ethics. Men are weak in the flesh and women like you prey upon them and lure them into your world of lust and vile sinful debauchery. This is your fault and you will be held accountable in this world and the next.

He is sorry that he ever met you and understands now that you are just pure trash and you have been leading him down a path toward evil and Hell's fury. He is repenting and wants nothing more to do with you.

So, again I say to you, stay away from my husband, or I will kill you. That is not a threat, it is a promise. Stay away or die.

Amelia Poindexter

I almost laughed, but it was still frightening. Who likes to be threatened with murder, but really, I lured him? All my fault? How stupid is this woman? What a load of crap he must be feeding her. What is it about women that make them swallow hook, line and sinker the stories their men tell them? Desperation I suppose, to hold onto something they think is valuable.

Well I reckon like gravity, what goes up must come down, and that includes my business and my personal life too. No more Noir to take the edge of my nerves with her strong, soft tongue. No more Garrett with his muscular body and his nice needle kit with the beautiful drugs of enhancement. No more Elle with her beautiful pussy and its luxuriant bush to twine my fingers through. And probably no more business after the I.R. S. gets through with me.

I decided to call Elle and see if she could help me get ready for this audit and figure out a plan of action. After all, she does owe me a lot. She may have earned a living on her back, but it was under my roof.

It was thrilling just to hear her voice, even though I'd had to go through three secretaries to get to her.

"Roxy, hello. It's wonderful to hear from you."

"Elle, thank you for talking to me. I know you're busy so I'll get right to the point. Remember how you used to help me with my bookkeeping? You were always so good with the numbers and the columns and such."

"Yes, I remember that," Elle answered, sounding a little puzzled.

"Well, I received notice today of an I.R.S. audit that goes back over the last three years and I was wondering if you would be willing to come over and help me get ready. I don't know where to begin. Please?"

"Roxy, I'm in the middle of a big case right now. How about Noir. Could she help you?"

"You know she's not with me any more, Elle. She's still with her big deal Hip Hop record producer. I haven't talked to her in ages and besides, she knows nothing about accounting. Which reminds me. The audit says I have to bring all my employee records too." I thought that might shake her up a little and get her attention. Miss Big Deal Downtown Legal Eagle.

I heard the unmistakable rustling of papers and then she answered, "All right then, I'll come over this weekend and see what I can do. I can't promise anything though, Roxy. I warned you about keeping two sets of books. You know I did."

"Uh huh, well thanks. I'll see you Saturday. We can have breakfast on the terrace like we used to. It'll be nice, you'll see."

Elle hung up without even answering me, but I felt better already. At least she was coming over. Maybe she could do a little something to help me relieve the tension that had been building in my belly for weeks, since the last time Garrett had been over and did a half-assed job of satisfying me. He was grinning like a jackass when he left, his pecker as limp as a noodle, but I could have used a lot more 'man with a slow hand' like the song lyrics. His wife is a fool. I lured him. Yeah, right. He always got the better 'end' of the deal.

I spent the next few hours going through my desk, trying to get my paperwork in some kind of order. One of the things I came across was my Last Will and Testament, executed years ago. Reading it brought back memories, sad thoughts, and the realization that we are all mortal.

Thinking about mortality also made me remember a session I once had with a remarkable psychic.

I was driving to my condo in Palm Bay and decided to take a little side trip to Cassadaga, Florida. I've always had a fascination with psychics and the occult. Since as far back as I can recollect, I've been able to sort of see things coming and know what was going on even when I wasn't there. I think that's one reason I've always been so successful as a whore; I just seem to know what people want and I give it to them. Maybe if I had spent more time developing my abilities, I would have made money fucking with people's minds rather than their bodies, but what are you gonna do. What's done is done.

Anyway, I followed the map off of Interstate 4 and found the little town, a village really, that has had a camp of psychics since the late 1800's. I parked and just stood on the sidewalk near the bookstore, letting my instincts guide me. I felt an overwhelming pull toward a small cottage in the historic camp with a discreet sign that read: Spiritualist and Certified Medium.

I knocked on the door and was greeted and invited inside by a woman of about fifty with salt and pepper hair and a very soft voice. She was the last thing you would expect a psychic medium to look like and I wondered if she was the housekeeper.

"No," she said, even though I had not voiced the question. "I am Sister Shelby. I've been expecting you."

Well, color me shocked and slap me silly. She was expecting me?

"Nice to meet you, Sister," I said, "but I didn't even know I was coming until I turned off the road. How the hell could you know I was coming?"

"You have special gifts, my dear. Come and have a seat and we will talk."

I spent the rest of the afternoon with the good woman, and learned a lot, both about myself and about what she called my special talents.

At the end of the day, the shadows were falling across her neat and orderly living room, and she stood and took my hand as I prepared to get back on the road to Palm Bay.

"Trust your instincts," she said. "And never doubt yourself. You know more than you think to know. You have been ignoring your insights for a long time and that must stop. You are my psychic sister and we are related in the spirit world. Beware of more."

"More what?" I asked her, confused.

She didn't answer, only smiling kindly. When I tried to pay her, she refused the money, smiling again, and ushering me out the door. As I left her porch, I noticed that she closed her blinds and turned off her porch light, letting folks with no psychic abilities of their own know that she was off duty for the evening.

Chapter 18

Here Pussy, Pussy, Pussy

After hanging up from speaking with Roxy, Elle cleared her office of interns, assistants, and clerks, and quickly placed a call to Stu. She and Stu had always kept in touch, even long after marrying Harrison. He had long since become a father figure in her life; someone she could trust and rely upon for honest answers and to be an ally. The sex they sometimes engaged in, in Elle's mind, didn't preclude the father figure status, as sex and fathers were inevitably intertwined in her psyche.

"Butler Security Systems," he answered.

"Stu, it's me. Can you talk?"

"Sure, doll baby. What's up besides my pecker?"

"Very funny. This is serious. I just got a strange call from Roxy. She wants me to come over there and help her prepare for an I.R.S. audit. Do you know anything about that?"

"Yeah, she mentioned it, and I'm not surprised. Like I told her, it could just be a random computer generated hit, or she could have been targeted by someone. Garrett's crazy wife perhaps. She also told me she got a threatening letter from the bitch. I suggest you be careful. Roxy's business is pretty tangled up."

"I will. Now tell me again, how's that big gun of yours?" She smiled as she said it and sipped tea from a china cup, looking admiringly around her beautiful office. She had hired a professional decorator, a man with long blonde hair who called himself Sparkle, and he had done a fantastic job. Her desk alone cost nearly ten thousand dollars.

"Still firing, baby doll. Loaded for bear. You interested? That rich Republican you married not gettin' the job done?"

"Oh, he's fine. He does what he can but you know I have a libido the size of Texas and he's just Rhode Island. Now you, on the other hand . . ."

"We'll make a date soon and I'll see if I can bring a smile to that pretty face of yours. Now you be careful of Roxy. She ain't beyond grabbing onto folks and takin' 'em down with her if she falls off a goddamn cliff."

"I'll be careful, but she's got nothing she can use against me, Stu. When I left the mansion I took everything I could find that might link me to the business. I wanted to start fresh and clean with Harrison and my law license."

She didn't mention to him that someone had been sending her pieces of jade stones with cryptic notes that she had never been able to figure out. She had no idea who was sending them or what they meant, but somehow the whole thing had felt threatening. There was no way, however, that she could go to the police without explaining who or what 'Jade' meant.

"Well, doll face, it's time you knew something then, but you gotta promise not to let Roxy know I told you this. A big part of my business is client trust, just like yours, both past and present."

"I promise, Stu. What is it for God's sake?"

"Roxy had me install a video monitoring system in the mansion a long time ago. There are cameras in every room, including her office, and they are voice activated. Once the camera comes on, so does the video taping system. That woman has got all of you on tape - a library that includes you, Noir and Roxy, me and you, and everything else you ever done."

"Oh, dear God, really? Stu, that could ruin me. Do you think she would blackmail me with that if she got in trouble with the government?"

"I honestly don't think she would, but you never know. People will do strange things when their back is against the wall. You just be careful and don't let her know you know. It may not be any big deal, this audit. She may grease right through it and be fine. Don't panic now. And if push comes to shove, I'll get them goddamn tapes back if I have to burn that place down or kill Roxy to do it. I've got your back, girlie."

"Thanks for letting me know about all this, Stu. And thanks for being on my side, but I don't think threats against Roxy are necessary at this point. That's not like you. Besides, she's done a lot for me over the years. She was good to me and I made a lot of money at *Hot'lanta Belles*. So be nice."

"Yeah, right. I'll be nice as long as she don't mess with you. She does that and she's gonna be sorry, that's all I'm sayin'."

"All right then. I'll keep you posted. I've gotta go. My voice mail light is blinking and people are knocking on my door. I love you, Stu."

"Love you too, baby doll."

Elle hung up, listened to her voice mails, then called her staff back in for a continuation of their strategy meeting for another big retail clothing store merger.

Saturday dawned bright and sunny; spring in Atlanta is a visual lesson in the beauty and renewal of life. The green hills and drama of lacy pink and white dogwood blossoms always reminded Elle of a stately, beautiful woman donning jewelry for a new season.

Pulling up to the mansion, Elle was once again impressed by the elegance of the stone façade and the gorgeous landscaping. It seemed, though, that there was a little hint of shabbiness here and there, but perhaps her standards had just risen since the Whitmire properties were always so meticulously maintained. Even though *Cherokee Falls* had miles of white fencing, it was constantly being freshly painted and the linear hedges clipped daily.

She rang the bell and was shown immediately to the terrace where Roxy was waiting with a lovely table set with fresh flowers, a silver tea service, and a colorful display of sliced fruit. Roxy, Elle thought, looked as beautiful as ever. Her green eyes and lustrous blonde hair gave her the look of a wealthy matron about to set off on a yacht cruise. She wore sparkling white silk slacks and a lime green silk blouse that emphasized the image of classic good taste. No one seeing her leaning against the carved balustrade would think she was a very experienced whore.

"Jade, come in! It's so great to see you," Roxy exclaimed, pulling Elle to her and hugging her tightly.

"It's good to see you too, Roxy. You look as beautiful as ever. You haven't changed one bit."

"You are such a liar! Thanks though. Sit down. Have some coffee so we can talk."

Elle noticed that there was a portable file box sitting ominously next to the table but she decided to ignore it as long as possible.

"How have you been?" Elle asked her former madam.

"Fine I suppose, but it seems like I keep losing things. Noir, you, Garrett. Now this goddamn audit. And business has been kind of slow. I think there are so many women giving it away these days, men aren't as willing to pay for a good piece of ass as they used to be. You know?"

"I do know, Roxy. That's too bad, but I'm sure you'll be just fine. You know these moral issues always go through cycles. You're probably just caught in one of the down turns. I wouldn't worry if I were you. Men will always be men. Now, tell me about this audit. I want to help you if I can, I'm just not sure how much I remember about what we did."

You don't need to remember, Roxy thought. *It's all on my wonderful state-of-the-art taping system.*

They spent most of the afternoon going through Roxy's red ledger books - there was one for each year that contained accounts payable, accounts receivable, expenses, payroll, and miscellaneous entries.

This set of books was the 'official' set meant for just such a purpose, which showed maximum expenses and minimum income, with the income purported to be from a bed and breakfast inn, the cover business for the mansion. Of course, this prohibited taking such business expense deductions as vibrators, condoms, costumes, dominatrix gear, and other accoutrements of the sex trade. Also non-deductible were the cash bribes paid to politicians for looking the other way, and the freebies given to law enforcement officers.

Elle looked through the employee files and was relieved to see that she had provided a false Social Security number when she first applied, so that would not lead back to her. But she was still concerned about the tapes showing her engaged in explicit sex acts with men, women, and sometimes entire groups. She squirmed a bit, remembering the escapades with Noir and Roxy and how exciting they had been. *Ahhh, those were the days*, she thought.

As Elle prepared to leave, having assured Roxy that her books seemed pretty well done and should withstand an ordinary I.R.S. audit with no problem, Roxy hugged her close, slipping her hand under Elle's skirt and sliding it between her legs. She felt the cool texture of narrow bikini panties that didn't stand a chance of containing Elle's long thick pubic hair. She tugged at a strand of hair and was aware of Elle's sudden sharp intake of breath.

"Roxy, stop," Elle said, pushing her hand away, but there was little conviction in her voice.

"Aw, come on, Jade, just once more for old time's sake? You know I've always loved your body. Come on upstairs just for a few minutes. It'll be fun." She slipped her hand back under the skirt, this time drawing her thumb across the crotch of the panties.

Elle was tempted, quite tempted actually, and could feel the dampness between her legs in response to Roxy's warm touch. Her knees went weak. It had been a long time since she had enjoyed a woman's tongue . . .

"I, I can't, Roxy. I've gotta go." She rushed out the door pushing her skirt down, pulling her car keys from her purse. She knew that if she delayed even a minute she would find herself rolling around on the floor with Roxy, lost in a hedonistic orgy of tongues, breasts, fingers and flailing arms and legs. There was no longer room in her life for that kind of abandonment. After all, she was married to a United States Senator, for God's sake.

As she pulled away from the mansion, she looked at herself in the rearview mirror, noting that her cheeks were bright red and her eyes had the glassy look of someone on the edge of some very bad behavior. She hoped Harrison was ready to play their favorite little game tonight - the one where he was the stallion and she was the fairy princess.

The next day Elle found herself sore after a vigorous game of riding the stallion with Harrison; he had outdone himself and Elle wondered if he was somehow enhancing himself with those little blue pills that seemed to be so popular. He had been insatiable and had indeed ridden her long and hard. The southern expression was 'rode hard and put away wet' and that was exactly how she felt.

She needed it though, after that tantalizing interlude with Roxy. She'd come close to giving in but was proud of herself for once for doing the right thing and going home to screw her husband's brains out. He had even gone down on her quite vigorously, which was not something he normally did. She usually had to tempt him with honey or whipped cream - one time she spread peanut butter all over her coochie and being a good old Southern boy, he had lapped that up.

"Nothing like a diet of pussy and protein," he had said, smacking his lips.

She had thought that the little gold labia ring she had would encourage him more, but food seemed to be the ticket. The way to a man's heart and all that.

"Whatever works, dear. Just so you eat it up," she had replied, watching his head bob up and down between her legs.

She tried reaching Noir all day Sunday but to no avail, then finally reached her at *Durty South Records* late Monday morning.

"Noir, it's Jade. We need to talk."

"About what, girl? You know I ain't with Roxy no more."

"I'm not either, Noir. But something's come up that I think you need to know about. Can we get together?"

"You not lookin' for free pussy are you? 'Cause I got a steady man now and he don't like me messin' with nobody else."

"No, Noir, this has nothing to do with sex. It's about business. Yours and mine. Do you want to meet with me or do you want to just stay ignorant and take your fucking chances?" She was getting on Elle's nerves with the street lingo. She knew damn good and well that Noir could sound like a college professor if she wanted to.

"Okay, okay, don't get your panties in a wad. Where and when?"

"Why don't you meet me for lunch in the Omni Hotel's Prime Meridian restaurant? I've got a meeting later in the afternoon in the CNN building and that would save me another trip downtown. I'll buy."

"Okay, tomorrow at twelve. See you there."

Elle arrived first and asked the Maitre D' to hold a table by one of the blue glass floor to ceiling windows with a view of Centennial Olympic Park. She had no idea what to expect with Noir, but was pleasantly surprised. She was wearing a beautifully tailored business suit, although she wore no blouse under it. The two-button jacket closed just beneath her breasts and a large solitaire diamond rested at the top of her luscious cleavage. It was a very classy yet sexy look and heads turned to watch her walk confidently toward Elle, her breasts moving in cadence with her stride. Her hair had so many extensions Elle couldn't imagine how it didn't give her a headache. She looked a bit like down-town Foxy Brown, but still beautiful in a hip urban kind of way. Although there was no hint of her athletic abilities, Elle couldn't help but picture her bending to snatch up a coin and make it disappear.

"Noir, you look beautiful, as always. I've got a table for us back there," Elle said, pointing to a secluded table toward the rear of the room.

"Thanks, Jade. You lookin' pretty good your own self," Noir replied, following Elle and the haughty Maitre D' to the table where creamy orchids, water and menus had already been placed. "You thinkin' I was gonna embarrass you, why you stuck us here in the back of the bus?"

"Good God, Noir. Of course not. I just don't want anyone to overhear our conversation. In case you're not aware of it, I'm pretty high profile now and reporters are always sniffing around looking for a story. My husband's a senator."

"Yeah, I know. I do read the papers. Me and Fabulous, we pretty *high profile* our own damn selves. Got to watch who we hang with. Like crooked ass politician's wives and such." She glanced over the menu, slammed it shut, took a sip of water leaving a blackberry lipstick stain on the rim, and said, "Now, why don't you get to the point, huh? Why we here?"

"You know, Noir, your attitude is a bit strange. I thought we were friends. We certainly know each other's bodies better than most married couples. In fact, I was just wondering when I saw you walk in if the lunch could possibly be as delicious as you look.

"So let's just try to make this a nice lunch, okay? We'll order first, then I'll tell you what I've found out about our friend Roxy."

They each ordered salads - Elle chose the Thai Ginger Lime Chicken Salad; Noir requested the Souvlaki Greek Salad with Spanakopita Pillows and Feta Cucumber Yogurt Sauce on the side, primarily because she thought it would impress Elle - and sweetened iced tea. While they waited on their food, Elle began.

"Noir, it seems that Roxy has gotten herself into a bit of a mess with the Internal Revenue Service. She's being audited. Now, it may be nothing, or it may turn into a very big deal. She has been keeping two sets of books for years and has cheated the government out of thousands and thousands of tax dollars. They tend to frown on that. Remember Willie Nelson? They made his life a living hell."

"What's her damn tax problems got to do with me and you," Noir asked, drumming her blackberry stained two inch nails impatiently against the white table linens. Noir was working hard at projecting attitude with a capital A and she was succeeding.

"Maybe nothing. Maybe everything. See, if she gets backed into a corner, she's going to start trying to make deals. And in order to make deals, she has to give them something. What if she could give them two ex-hookers, both now very high profile, and both very interesting to government officials anxious to make a big splash in the media."

"She ain't got nothin' on me. I made sure when I left there I took everything with me. Pictures, everything. Plus, I gave her a fake Social Security number when she hired me, so it won't trace back to me. It would just be her word against mine. She would look desperate. My man got lawyers can handle shit like that, no sweat." She snapped her fingers and several diners turned to look over at them.

"Yeah, me too," Elle said, keeping her voice to a hissed whisper. "I took everything with me and gave a fake social too, but guess what? Roxy has been secretly video taping all of us, every room, every date, every john and saving the tapes for a rainy day. Do you think your mister Hip Hop mogul would like some video on television or on the internet showing his precious Noir fucking women? Or fucking two men at once, one in the pussy and one in the ass? How do you think he would react to that, Noir?"

Noir nearly choked on her iced tea and Elle thought she might cry. Her big chocolate brown eyes were suddenly swimming in tears. The attitude has gone to a small a, replaced by an endearing vulnerability.

"Oh, God, Jade, that would ruin everything for me. He would throw me out on my ass. He might even kill me. He got a fierce bad temper and his bodyguards carry guns. I've seen them beat the snot out of people for just looking at Fab the wrong way. What are we gonna do?"

She stared out the window and waited quietly, dabbing at her eyes with a napkin, while the waiter put their salads down, offered cracked pepper and grated parmesan cheese, then backed away from their table.

Elle thought about mentioning the pieces of jade with the mysterious notes she had been receiving, but decided against it. Noir didn't need to know about that, at least not yet. It may have nothing to do with the whole Roxy situation anyway.

As they nibbled their salads, each lost in their own thoughts, Elle's cell phone began to vibrate. The number read 'restricted', but she somehow sensed that she needed to take the call.

"Excuse me," she said to Noir, flipping open the phone. "Hello?"

A voice she didn't recognize said, "Don't worry, Jade. Everything will be all right. Daddy will take care of his baby. Shhhhh now. Daddy loves you." The call clicked off.

What the hell? Who was that? Daddy? My father has been dead for years. But he called me Jade!

Elle's mind whirred with possibilities but none of them made sense.

"What's wrong, girl?" Noir asked. "Your face done gone white as good coke. You okay?"

"Oh, sorry, Noir. Very strange call, that's all. Maybe a wrong number. Anyway, where were we?"

"We tryin' figure out what to do about Roxy and her fuckin' video tapes, that's what." She viciously stabbed a piece of lettuce and continued, "Listen, my man got people who can take care of this bitch, once and for all. I snap my fingers and they don't say 'how high?' they say 'on who?'. You just say the word, and trust me, Roxy can disappear. I'll just have to figure out a story to tell Fab, that's all, but I can do that no problem."

"Ummmm, well, I don't think we're to that point yet, but it's something to keep in mind. Why don't I just wait and see how her audit goes and we'll take it from there. She promised to keep me posted on what happens."

"Aw'ite then, we'll wait a bit, but we wait too long and she start givin' up names and shit and we'll be on the front page of the paper 'fore you can say 'fuck me'."

"I understand. I just don't want to jump the gun. I'll call you as soon as I know anything." Elle handed her a gold embossed business card with all of her numbers, both official and private, listed. "Be sure to call me if you hear anything before I do."

"I don't 'spect to hear anything in my world 'cept beat lyrics and bullshit, but I'll call you if I do." She pushed back from the table, blotted her glistening blackberry lips, and walked away, leaving Elle with the check and a tantalizing view of her beautiful ass, undulating between tables of admiring men.

Chapter 19

Things Don't Add Up

Two weeks had gone by and Elle had heard nothing from Roxy.
Why, she wondered? What had happened with the audit? The last
time Elle had spoken with Roxy she had suggested that she take a trip
down to her Palm Bay, Florida condominium home to relax for a bit.
Maybe Roxy had decided to just stay there, skip the audit, and maybe skip
out on everything. She certainly wouldn't be the first to run away from an
I.R.S. audit, Elle knew. She decided to call.

The phone at the mansion was answered by a male voice that Elle did
not recognize.

"May I speak with Miss Porter please?" Elle asked.

"Who, may I ask, is calling," asked the deep baritone voice.

"Just a friend. Is she there?"

"Well, Miss Friend, Roxanne Porter has gone missing. She is not
here. The mansion seems to have been abandoned. Perhaps you would
like to come over here and provide some information on her possible
whereabouts?"

"Certainly not. And who are you?"

"This is field agent Richard Carter of the Internal Revenue Service.
And I suggest that you reconsider your attitude. It's always better to
cooperate in these matters, especially when tax evasion may be involved.
Your cooperation now could go a long way toward clearing Miz Porter
and keeping her associates out of jeopardy."

Elle hung up immediately, glad that she had used a pay phone in the lobby of her office building. Thousands of people daily passed through this building and any one of them could have used this phone. She grabbed tissues from her purse and wiped her finger prints off the buttons and the receiver, and walked quickly away.

Where the hell was Roxy? And where were those damned video tapes?

She used her cell phone to call Noir and they agreed to meet again that night, this time at the *Durty South Recordings* condo in the Atlantic Station Development. Noir had a key and she assured Elle that no one else would be there. She would get things set up and send the housekeeper home for the night.

Elle was impressed with the condominium, especially the beautiful stone fireplace that dominated the room and gave it a warmth that would otherwise be lacking with the sleek contemporary furnishings. She loved the large white rug that lay before the fireplace and could picture herself and Harrison making love there. Or perhaps herself and Noir?

Her thoughts were interrupted by Noir's entrance.

"Hello again, Jade. Or should I call you Elle now? That's the name that was on your business card. Do you ever wonder who the real 'you' is? Jade or Elle? I sometimes wonder if I'm really plain old Lashonda from the projects or Noir, classy whore from some exotic island I've never been to."

"The truth is probably somewhere between the two, for both of us. I don't think we are ever only one thing. My daddy told me one time when I was about to take a long bus ride that life is like that bus ride. People enter and exit your life at different times and for different reasons. Sometimes it's for a season and sometimes its forever. Maybe our identities are like that too. They come and go and change as the journey continues."

"God, Girl, that's deep." She laughed and handed Elle a brightly colored calendar featuring twelve different pictures of herself.

"Noir, these are beautiful. Are these outfits from the *Durty Rags* collection?"

The cover featured a glistening Noir, her skin sparkling with gold dust, holding two sparklers strategically placed to hide her large brown nipples. Inside, there were month by month shots, from a wintry Noir in January faux fur to a Christmas Noir on Santa's lap. It was obvious from the photo of a grinning Santa that he was giving Noir a little Christmas gift from behind as she straddled him.

"Yes, and it's due to be released in November for the New Year. That's why I can't afford to have this shit with Roxy blow up in my face right now. It will ruin everything."

Once again Elle noticed the big eyes filling with tears. Whether real or fake, they were touching.

"Can we sit down? I've got some news and we need to figure out what it means."

"Kick off your shoes and let's stretch out on the rug. I've decanted a nice red wine here for us."

She poured two glasses of wine, handed one to Elle, and they both sat down cross-legged on the rug. They clinked glasses, giggling like school girls. Possibly because she was on her own turf, it seemed to Elle that Noir was a completely different person that the one she had met in the restaurant. She was friendlier, more relaxed.

"Here is to disproportionate wealth and prosperity for the world's comfort women," Noir said. "May they live to love, laugh, and fornicate forever!"

"Well said! Not quite as profound as my little story," said Elle, "but probably much more truthful."

As they both wiggled around and got comfortable, Elle continued, "Okay, here's what I know."

She went on to relate the story of calling the mansion, getting an I.R.S. agent on the phone, and finding out that Roxy was missing. She concluded by asking Noir if she knew anything about Roxy's disappearance.

"Hell naw," Noir replied quickly, sliding easily back into her street persona. "You said to wait so I've waited. I ain't said nothin' to nobody. Where you s'pose them video tapes are? We need to find 'em."

"Yes, we do," replied Elle. "And that's what I'm here to discuss."

"You got any ideas?"

"Well, the feds have obviously searched the mansion so if the tapes were there they've already found them and we're too late. But maybe Roxy took them with her. I think she probably went down to Florida. She has a condo in Palm Bay. Even if she's not there, maybe she hid the tapes and her secret set of books there. I think it's worth you and me going down there to take a look. Can you get away for a few days without Fabulous getting his dick in a knot?"

Noir couldn't help but laugh at the picture of Fabulous with his long skinny pecker tied in a knot, but she answered, "I can try. I'll make up some bullshit story about you a friend and your momma be in Florida and be sick. He a sucker for sick momma stories."

"Okay, the sooner the better. I can get my business squared away tomorrow, cancel appointments, tell Harrison some bullshit about taking a deposition in Florida, and we can go on Wednesday. I'll drive. How does that sound?"

"Sounds good, girl."

Noir got up and opened a second bottle of wine, refilled both of their glasses, and walked over to the door to make sure it was locked. The wine was kicking in, making her feel warm, silky and relaxed, and she didn't want the housekeeper or worse, Fabulous, to walk in.

"Now, how about you and me, for old time's sake, huh?"

She took a gulp of wine, sat the glass down on the hearth, and leaned over to kiss Elle, her tongue pushing deeply into Elle's throat. The force of the kiss pushed Elle onto her back immediately arousing her, and soon the two women were exploring each other's bodies with the enthusiasm of college girls in a first time lesbian encounter.

Their expensive outfits were tossed like rags around the perimeter of the room, Elle's bra knocking a nine hundred dollar vase to the floor, shattering it into thousands of pieces.

"Oops," she said, laughing, and offering a now freed breast to Noir, who took it hungrily into her mouth, sucking hard, nearly, but not quite, crossing the line between pleasure and pain.

Elle explored Noir's lithe and muscular body with her mouth, tasting and savoring every inch, as Noir twisted and contorted herself as always, providing Elle with different views and different access moment by moment.

After an hour of satiating each other with hands, tongues, and warm candlesticks, they both laid back on the furry rug, happy, relaxed, and more satisfied than either had been in a long time.

"So, does this mean we're friends again?" Elle asked, idly tracing around Noir's lovely nipples with a wine dampened finger.

"I reckon, girl," Noir replied, as Elle licked the droplets of wine from her breasts. "Now stop it and let me get dressed. Fab gonna be wondering where I am and I gotta have the energy left to fuck him tonight too, else he won't be in no mood to let me take off for Florida."

Elle reluctantly stood and began dressing. They parted with one more long, deep kiss, their thighs pressed together, and Elle drove home, her body feeling alternately relaxed and thrumming with excitement.

This trip to Florida should be fun, now that she and Noir were such good friends again. *Yum,* she thought.

Chapter 20

Holes in the Road to Perdition

*E*lle and Noir felt like movie runaways Thelma & Louise, heading out on their Florida road trip in Elle's Porsche Carrera GT convertible, hair flying and lustful intentions for each other's bodies ready to be unpacked at a moment's notice. They loved their men, in different ways and for different reasons, but their newly rediscovered excitement over each other's bodies made them feel like kids on Christmas morning with a beautiful package to unwrap.

Fabulous and Harrison had bought their stories and the girls had promised both men to call them frequently and to be careful on the trip.

After circling south on Atlanta's spider web 285 loop, they continued south on I-75, bound for Florida's sunshine and much flatter terrain. When they hit the east-west span of I-10, Elle took it eastbound, then switched to I-95 south, which would take them directly to Palm Bay on Florida's eastern coast. The trip would take at least eight hours but after stopping at a Denny's for lunch, Elle let Noir drive, glad to have the opportunity to lay her head back and rest her eyes. She had been up most of the night writing instructions and finishing up pleadings that had to be filed in court by her clerks. Even when she got in the shower to relax her neck muscles before going to bed, she wasn't allowed to rest, as Harrison had joined her for one of his lackluster quickie performances.

"Oh, God, Elle, I love you so much," he moaned and groaned, while she worked hard to make him come quickly so she could get to bed.

"Yes, I love you too, but could you hurry up? I'm so tired."

She touched a spot at the base of his penis that she knew drove him crazy, and within seconds he was finished, to her great relief.

As he did every time they made love, he bent down and kissed her belly. "Did we make a baby tonight?" he would coo in baby talk. "Daddy hopes so."

They never used any kind of birth control because Harrison desperately wanted a child to carry on the family name, wealth, and Whitmire legacy, but it just never happened. When he urged her to go to a specialist, she always put it off, telling him that it would happen when the good Lord wanted it to. That sentiment was frequently uttered by Harrison's mother, so he didn't doubt it for a moment. Not that Elle didn't want children, she did, eventually, but it just never seemed to be the right time.

Perhaps when all this was done with Roxy and the tapes were secure, and once she had gotten Noir out of her system, maybe then it would be time to worry about having a baby. But not now. Not when every time she closed her eyes she saw Noir's big black hairy pussy, winking at her, squeezing and relaxing, inviting, demanding her tongue to plunge its depths.

It was completely dark and a huge silvery moon hung low in the sky by the time they reached Palm Bay. They were both tired and bored with the billboard and tee shirt shop scenery and Noir turned into the first decent looking motel she saw.

The *Queen of the Reef* was a pink and turquoise homage to the old Florida motels of the 1950's, but it looked clean and had a sign out front boasting of triple-A membership and was apparently 'American owned'.

After checking in and then grabbing burgers at the fast food place next door, they decided to take a run over to Roxy's condo just to see if they could determine whether or not she was there. Sex would have to wait.

Elle knew the way; she had been down to Palm Bay several times as Roxy's companion. She knew that Roxy's unit was on the ground floor, rear south corner, with an ocean view. Elle still had a key but didn't want to use it if Roxy was there, fearing an unpleasant and hard to explain confrontation.

Walking slowly and pretending to be tourists out for an evening stroll, they followed the winding stone pathway around the building. When it began leading away from the building, they quickly and quietly veered off into the damp grass and stayed close to the hedges.

"Don't worry," Elle whispered to Noir. "Most of the residents here are a hundred fucking years old. They aren't going to be out walking around at ten o'clock at night."

"Yes, but a security guard might be," Noir responded.

As they came around the north corner of the building, that unit was dark and they were completely hidden from view. They reached the patio of Roxy's unit and saw that lights were on. They could hear voices but weren't sure if it was conversation or merely a television or radio.

Noir followed in Elle's footsteps as she crouched to get past the low window. Since the window to Roxy's living room faced the ocean, she hadn't bothered to close the curtains. They were able to peek in and see Roxy sitting in her underwear on the pale green sofa watching a video tape.

Elle had to clamp her hand over her own mouth to keep her from gasping aloud - the tape was one of her in a dominatrix outfit, whipping some client whose name she had long since forgotten. She couldn't even remember the guy's reason for wanting to be punished, but she thought he was a politician of some sort. Maybe a city council member. He was black with a thick moustache and the smallest penis Elle had ever seen. He looked like a four year old boy from the waist down. It was pathetic, but when you are in the business, you take them all on no matter what.

As they watched, Roxy took that tape out and put another one in, this one showing the three of them rolling around on the big round bed in Roxy's room at the mansion. Elle had never noticed how Roxy's huge silicone boobs stayed in place no matter what position she was in. *Funny what you notice when you watch yourself on television*, Elle thought, but she stayed quiet. She was furious to discover that Roxy had indeed secretly taped them; somehow she had been holding out hope that Stu was wrong.

After watching Roxy change tapes a few more times, she motioned to Noir to turn around and go back the way they had come. Watching all the action had definitely turned her on and she couldn't wait to get back to the motel room. She hoped Noir had been affected the same way. If not she would be spending some time with her favorite massager, which luckily she had remembered to pack.

On the way back to the motel, they discussed what to do about Roxy. Elle didn't mention it to Noir, but it looked to her like the set up Roxy had, with two VCRs, she had probably been making copies of the tapes as they watched her.

Noir was furious. "That bitch got us both on tape, our faces full front for the fucking world to see. We gotta do something, and do it fast, before those agents that raided her mansion figure out she down here in the land of sand and old farts."

"You're right, Noir. But what should we do? She needs to disappear. How can we make that happen? I know a private detective I can call if we need to. Remember Stu?"

"Yeah, I remember his honky ass, but let me make a couple of calls. I know some boys that can get rid of that back stabbing cunt."

She fished her cell phone out of her huge Louis Vuitton purse and dialed a number from memory.

"Yo, Slo Mo. S'up, man?" She listened for a moment then explained where they were and what they needed to have happen. "And, Slo Mo, you can bring Thug T to help you, but don't tell nobody else, 'specially not Fabulous, you got me? If you have to, you call in sick or somethin', but make it real. There's five big ones in it for you."

She turned to Elle, snapping her phone shut. "It's done. They be headin' this way tonight and they gonna take care of her. You got five grand you can give me for them? I can't get my hands on that kind of cash without Fab knowin' about it."

"Sure, as long as there are plenty of ATM's around here. I'll get the cash before we leave here but it'll take several machines."

They barely got the curtains pulled and the chain on the motel room door before Elle began pulling at Noir's clothes, trying to undress her. Apparently the tapes had affected Noir as much as they had Elle, because she popped the buttons on her newest *Durty Rags* top trying to get it off.

The housekeeper knocking at the motel room door woke Elle. She opened her eyes and realized that she had fallen asleep with her head on Noir's thigh, so the first thing she saw was Noir's bush, up close and personal. She couldn't help but smile, remembering the night before. It had been everything she had hoped for, and more. They had both been driven into a fury of passion by the video tapes, which not only drove them to fuck each other's brains out, but confirmed their belief that the tapes needed to be destroyed.

"Come back later," she yelled, and the knocking stopped.

She nuzzled her face against Noir, then untangled herself, took a shower, and then made coffee in the little machine conveniently placed there by the hotel management. A Styrofoam cup of mediocre coffee would have to do, but she much preferred her usual triple shot grande latte from the StarBucks in her office building.

She was on her third cup when Noir finally roused, smiling when she saw Elle sitting in the orange motel chair, nude, her leg thrown casually over the arm of the chair.

"Good God, girl, you trying to drive me crazy? Cover that thing up."

She tossed a pillow at Elle nearly spilling her coffee, and went to the bathroom. Elle heard the toilet flush then the shower start. She smiled, put down her coffee, and joined Noir in the shower. She poured shampoo into her hands and used the vanilla scented lather to rub all over Noir's body, then she made Noir stand on the sides of the tub. Elle got on her knees and began to lap at Noir's pussy, causing the girl to moan and bounce up and down against her face.

Soon they left the awkward shower, both soaking wet, and went back to the bed where they had better access to each other and could use some of the toys that Elle had brought. There was a jar of imported honey, a double sided dildo, and of course, their own tongues and fingers.

By the time they were both sated, the room was a mess and ants were already beginning to march toward the honey smeared bedspread.

"I guess we better check out of here and find somewhere else to stay," Elle said laughing. "You have left pussy tracks from one side of this room to the other."

"Me? Them's your pussy tracks, girl. But I gotta say, Elle, you still taste fine. Roxy always bragged about you tastin' like caviar but I'd never had caviar so I didn't know what she meant. But now I do and she right. You taste good, girl. Um, um good."

"Thanks, Noir. You taste damn fine yourself. Better than any pecker I ever tasted, that's for sure."

They packed up their things and left the room, turning the door knob hanger toward 'Clean, Please', and went to find breakfast. Suddenly they were both famished and wanted something that tasted more like eggs than caviar.

After a filling breakfast of omelets, pancakes and bacon at the strip mall's Shoreline Café, they decided to spend some time shopping and then they planned to lie out on the beach for a while. They wanted to stay close to make sure Noir's boys got the job done and no problems arose. After Roxy was taken care of, they would go into the condo and get rid of the tapes.

By six o'clock they were both sun and wind burned and bored. They wanted to either get another motel room or head to Roxy's and get things finished. Harrison had called Elle's cell phone twice and Fabulous called Noir damn near every hour, asking how her friend's sick momma was. They were both getting tired of lying and tired of getting hit on at the beach. Elle's untamed bush - she still never shaved or waxed - could not be confined by her miniscule pink string bikini, and caused stares and spontaneous erections up and down the beach, and Noir was stunning in a white lace one-piece suit with a key-hole cut out that featured her belly button ring and flattered her curves. When she saw anyone looking at her, male or female, she squeezed and released her pussy muscles making her bathing suit material dance.

Noir called Slo Mo's cell phone and for the first time that day, he answered.

"Yo, speak."

"Slo Mo, it's Noir. Are we cool?"

"Yeah, we cool, 'cept we didn't do nothin'."

"What? What does that mean? Why didn't you take care of her?"

"Bitch wasn't there, that's why. We even went in and looked around. She gone. We headed back north. You still gotta pay me, yo, 'cause we tried. It ain't our fault the bitch be gone. You done wasted our valuable time."

"Oh, fuck," said Noir. "Yeah, just keep your mouth shut and I'll pay you anyway. You best not be tryin' to git over on me, that's all I'm sayin'." She snapped her phone shut.

"What happened?" Elle asked, her brows knit together with concern.

"Those two stupid niggas said she's not there. Her place is empty. Where could she have gone?"

"I don't know. Maybe they never even came down here and are lying. I've got a key. We'll go see," Elle replied, making an illegal U-turn on A1A. Horns honked but she just shot them a bird and floored it. Thelma and Louise weren't about to take shit from these old snow birds driving their twenty year old Cadillac sedans twenty miles an hour.

They parked on the far end of the parking lot at the condo building and went around to Roxy's sliding glass patio door to take a peek inside. They saw nothing; everything was quiet. They decided to go inside, tried the door, and found it unlocked.

"Roxy? Anybody home," Elle called out.

There was no answer. She and Noir stood in the middle of the room they had watched Roxy in just the night before, but it was as still and quiet as if it had never been inhabited.

The room was clean and neat; they could even see vacuum cleaner tracks on the white carpeting. The room smelled of lemon furniture polish, and something else. Something vaguely reminiscent of . . . what?

Iron? Blood?

"Noir, I smell blood. I'm sure of it. Did those guys you sent over here say anything about blood?"

"No. They just said she wasn't here, that's all. Those dumb asses, if they . . ."

"Never mind. You go that way and check the kitchen and utility room and I'll go check the bedrooms. Yell if you find anything. This is creepy."

They each tip toed across the floor, stepping lightly as though they feared something, they just didn't know what. Was something going to jump out at them? Noir had seen all the Halloween movies and she knew what could happen to two beautiful young women in a dark apartment all alone.

"Elle," she called out, "I don't s'pose you got a gun?"

"Shut up, Noir. Of course I don't have a gun. Just look around. Look for the tapes or for what stinks in here. If Roxy jumps out of a closet, we'll have a good laugh and that will be it."

Elle opened the guest bedroom closet and behind the vacuum cleaner she spotted a yellow carrying case with a black handle. She pulled it out.

"Noir, I found the tapes," she yelled. "I just hope this is all of them."

Noir came back to the bedroom to see and visually counted at least thirty tapes.

"Who the hell knows how many she had. Keep looking. There may be more. I'll go check the bathroom."

When she got to the bathroom, she screamed again for Elle. "Oh, God, Elle, git in here. Now!"

There was blood everywhere. On the sink, the floor, the marble countertop, and in the shower.

"Shit," said Elle, "it looks like somebody slaughtered a pig in here."

"If this is Roxy's blood, then where the hell is Roxy?" Noir whispered.

"Go back out front," Elle ordered, "and look in all the closets. I'll check both bedrooms again, then we gotta get the hell out of here."

Searching Roxy's desk, Elle found what looked like Roxy's address book. It was a small, red leather bound book which Elle slipped into her pocket to read later.

After a thorough look under beds and in closets and finding no body and no Roxy hiding from them, Elle and Noir took the case of tapes and left, leaving the door unlocked as they had found it.

Once they were back on the interstate, this time headed north, Elle stopped at a roadside convenience store and called 9-1-1 and anonymously reported suspicious noises coming from Unit 101, Seaside Condominiums. She clicked off quickly, hopefully before they could get a read on the phone number.

Where the hell is Roxy?, Elle wondered. *Where did all that blood come from? And what the hell is on all these tapes?*

Chapter 21

Submarines and Things That Go Deep

I made a huge mistake leaving those tapes in my condo, but we ran out of time and losing lots of blood can make a girl real light headed. I had decided to bring everything down to Florida after getting that nasty threatening letter from Garrett's stupid wife. Better safe than sorry I always say. Like the psychic told me, I was now listening to my gut instincts. Hopefully, I wasn't too rusty to save myself.

What no one knew was that I also own the condo across the hall, which is where we hid, keeping an eye on the parade of people visiting me. After those thugs came, I knew things were serious and I had to make some decisions.

See, a long time ago I met one of my Nashville mansion clients, because he had a special interest in Jade. He thought we should work together in her best interest and I agreed. He seemed both quite sincere in his love for her, and just crazy enough to make me pay close attention and want to keep him an ally. Looking back, my instincts were perfectly on target, as usual. No madam worth her salt doesn't know how to read people. Without that ability, you don't stay in business for very long. Finding out I have other special abilities was icing on the cake.

This man lived in Rome, Georgia and became a Nashville client after the love of his life left his home for college. He was devastated, he missed her, and he hoped that one of my girls could take her place in his bed and in his heart.

The manager, a very smart woman named Evelyn, felt sorry for him. He couldn't even get it up with most of the girls, and showed little or no interest in any of them. They were all too old, he said, and too experienced. He was turned on by youth and innocence. She decided to ask me to come up there in a last ditch effort to find him some barely legal pussy so as not to lose a potentially good client. It became a challenge for her.

So I went up to Nashville and spent an entire weekend, showing him the catalogs from my other mansions to see if any of the girls turned him on.

He flipped through the books with a disinterested attitude, like you'd flip the magazine pages in a doctor's office, but when he saw the picture of Jade, he jumped up and yelled excitedly, pointing to the page, "Oh, my god, that's her. That's my baby doll. She's working for you? She's a whore?"

He was barely making sense, but it was obvious he had some kind of connection to Jade. He got a very obvious hard on just looking at the picture, and he couldn't get one with a real live pussy in his face. Not even mine, which I have to tell you, is pretty damn nice. I built a multi-million dollar business on it, in fact.

"She works for me, yes. But don't call her a whore. My girls are professionals that provide a valuable service. They are talented experts. Do you understand me, sir? Don't call them whores!"

For an answer I got a somewhat contrite nod, but he stared at Jade's picture for a long time. It was one that my photographer had taken, showing her in a cheerleader outfit, her hair pulled up into two bouncy pony tails. She looked innocent, smiling at the camera, but as always with Jade, there was an underlying tone of sensuality that the camera captured perfectly. She was sucking her thumb and had her other hand between her legs.

I had to tell him that this girl was located in Atlanta and was a college student, so she could not come up to Nashville. I also discouraged that kind of thing - cross pollinating - I liked to keep the businesses physically and geographically separated, with separate sets of books. In rare cases I would move girls around, but I didn't do it often and his need didn't seem to qualify. He just wanted to fuck somebody that looked as innocent as a child. That was his hot button.

He said he understood, but something told me that he was not going quietly away. He had no plans to let this go. His eyes had gotten a feverish look in them and his hands shook as his finger traced Jade's outline. Again, my instincts were dead on.

We parted company but two weeks later, he called me. He wanted to know all about Jade - where she lived and where she worked. He said he felt a fatherly concern for her and wanted to make sure she was protected. Even though he threatened me, I refused to give him any information. That can be dangerous for my girls and I just don't do it. Men frequently get infatuated with working girls and want to 'take them away' from the business. They refuse to accept the fact that my girls work for me because they want to, not because they are forced into some kind of servitude.

I promised him that I would watch out for her and would let him know if she ever needed anything. For a while he called regularly, always asking about Jade, and from time to time I sent him pictures of her. She never knew about any of this; I couldn't see worrying her and he seemed harmless enough. One time he sent her a package at the mansion and I opened it. It was a baby doll dressed in pink knit clothes and sucking on a bottle. I gave it to my housekeeper Marta to take home to her children and never told Jade.

Then one day he just stopped calling.

But he didn't go away; he just went deep and quiet, staying below the surface like a submarine. His name was Ted Moore.

I hadn't heard from Ted Moore for two years. Then he showed up at my condo the same night the thugs from Atlanta came after me.

I was in my second condo, Unit 102, watching the hallway through the peep hole in my door, when I saw him knock on Unit 101. At first, since the peep hole distorts images, I didn't recognize him. He had aged a little and put on some weight, but I never forget a face so when he turned to make sure no one else was in the hallway, I got a good look. It was him all right. What the hell did he want? And what a night to show up.

I had been reviewing tapes and making notes, getting ready for my I.R.S. audit and making sure I had enough ammunition to fight back with. That was what my attorney had suggested. He said the only way to get the I.R.S. sharks off my scent was to feed them chum. Unfortunately, and I hated doing it, but Noir and Elle were going to be my chum.

Now, don't get me wrong. I loved those girls and ordinarily would not do a thing to harm them. But this was a matter of life and death for me. If I got sucker punched by the feds, and they started talking Rico Act, I needed to give them something else to gnaw on. My business might still be done for, but maybe I could avoid jail and poverty. That was my hope, anyway.

So now things get a bit more complicated. Somebody's trying to kill me, and psycho Ted Moore is knocking on my door. What's a girl to do? Well, as they say, when opportunity knocks, open the door.

"Ted Moore?" I whispered, opening the door a crack.

He spun around and saw me peeking out from behind the security chain.

"Yes, Roxy? Did I get the wrong apartment?"

"Not really, I own both. Hang on and let me undo this chain."

I shut the door, unlatched the chain, and opened the door wide enough for him to come in. I kept one hand in the pocket of my robe, clutching the pepper spray I always keep handy.

"What are you doing here? What do you want?" *What a fucking night,* I thought for the umpteenth time.

"Roxy, I've been watching your place, actually I was following Jade, and I saw those thugs leave. I also saw Jade and some black girl go through your place across the hall and leave with a big yellow container of some sort. I thought I better check on you, see if you were okay. Lots of comings and goings for a quiet Florida condo by the ocean, wouldn't you say?"

"Yes, it's been quite a night. I've been hiding over here. No one knows I own this unit. The two black men I'm pretty sure came to kill me, and the girls took some video tapes I've been secretly keeping. It's a long story, but thank God I'm okay. At least for now. Mind telling me why you're on Jade's tail?"

"What are the bandages on your arms for then, if you're okay?" Ted asked me, ignoring my question. "And your robe; is that blood?"

"Oh, that. Yes, I need to change but I don't have any clothes over here. I kind of accidentally on purpose cut my wrists and left a lot of blood in that condo," I replied, pointing across the hall. "I wanted the girls to think I was maybe dead so they would go away. It worked I think, but they can't figure out where my body is." I had to laugh, thinking about them searching for my cold dead body. Knowing Noir, she was probably scared shitless. She loves horror movies mainly because they scare her. I've been dealing with whores most of my life, and it's my theory that they get hardened to their own emotions. Even something as silly as a scary movie sort of awakens them and takes away the numbness. But what do I know? I'm just a madam!

"That's kind of drastic isn't it? You could have bled to death."

"Listen, I've seen suicides before and I know how much the wrists bleed. I was careful but I had to make it look real. It's a chance I was willing to take. My life is on the line and if I don't do something, I'm gonna be dead for real. Those men meant business and if I hadn't been able to slip out the patio door I'd be dead meat right now."

I had Ted run across the hall and bring me some clothes, and not a minute after he got back inside, the cops showed up and banged loudly on my door. The girls must have called them after seeing all that blood.

When no one answered, they went in, guns drawn. Fortunately, they left the door standing open so I could watch through the peep hole as they searched the apartment. I heard one of them yelling about finding blood in the bathroom and soon they had called for a forensics team and some back up.

It scared the shit out of me when they banged on the door to my secret second unit, but I just slid down to the floor and motioned for Ted to be quiet. I was terrified that Cooter would bark, but he behaved himself.

Once the detectives and some guys with large cases arrived, the patrolmen began their canvas, knocking on other doors. I knew they'd get no information. Most of the residents here are old and deaf and wouldn't have heard anything if I'd been raped, murdered and screamed my head off. I also knew that soon enough they would figure out that I owned two condos in the building, so Ted Moore and I took off together like thieves in the night, just me, him and my precious little Cooter, flying north in his big SUV. Maybe it's the Southern girl in me, but I just love a man with a big ol' truck, but I still hated to abandon my own beautiful little Benz convertible, but it's too recognizable, too distinctive, so we left it in a strip mall parking lot, looking like a diamond in a bowl of oatmeal. It made me sad, but I kept telling myself I would come back for her, and I was really hoping I'd be able to.

Unfortunately, Ted wasn't the least bit interested in me or my feelings, just in what was going on with Jade, so we decided to head straight for the Atlanta mansion. I wasn't sure at all what his real motives were. Why had he been following Jade? I asked again but he didn't explain; just said he was looking out for her like he always did. There was a lot I didn't know, but he seemed all right with going to *Hot'lanta Belles* and figuring out our next steps. It didn't seem to make sense to sit around Palm Bay and get questioned by a bunch of stupid cops.

"So, tell me what's going on with you and Jade," Ted asked me, once we were cruising easily and out of the city traffic. Cooter was curled up in the back seat sound asleep.

"Nothing," I said. "She doesn't work for me any more. She's a big deal attorney and married to that snooty senator now. Why are you followin' her around?"

Once again he ignored my question and asked one of his own.

"Then why did she go to the mansion last week and why did she follow you down here?"

"I am not answering any more of your questions until you answer mine. Now you tell me right fuckin' now why you followed Jade."

"That's none of your business, and if you're smart you'll not make me any madder than I already am. We're going straight to that whore house of yours and I'm going to find out what's going on with my Jade. Daddy always takes care of his girls and that's all you need to know."

I was beginning to think I had made a big mistake taking off with this lunatic and couldn't wait to get Stu to run a background check on him. I decided to call him as soon as we got to Atlanta.

We made one pee and coffee stop at a golden arches and were in Atlanta by four o'clock. Ted kept reciting nursery rhymes and humming 'Rock a By Baby'. I was dead tired and just wanted to crawl in the bed but things had gone to hell while I had been away.

The mansion was as dark and deserted as a witch's cunt, and I always made sure it was blazing with lights and filled with music. No one was around; not one single girl or housekeeper. Mail was piled up on the hallway credenza and my adrenaline had kicked in enough so that I took it into my office and began sorting through it.

There was a subpoena from the I.R.S. for document production and I had missed the deadline date while I was in Florida. Damn that Jade to hell for giving me that advice. And there were bills totaling thousands of dollars that I didn't have, thanks to the place having no business going on. My bank account had been frozen. This was a nightmare.

Ted Moore wandered around, sipping a beer from the kitchen, and listening to me cuss. I was not being very lady like for sure.

I called my attorney, knowing I would get his goddamn voice mail, but I had to do something. I couldn't just let this be. I told him in no uncertain terms that I wanted to do whatever I had to do to appease the government so they'd back out of my life. If that meant giving them Noir, Jade, my customer lists that included cops, GBI agents, and some other alphabet soup agents, so be it. I told him to set it up and I'd be in his office first thing tomorrow morning.

Someone called my name, and as I hung up the phone I turned toward the door. There was a deafening noise in the quiet room, a tremendous hot pain in my chest, and then darkness.

As I laid there on the floor of my office, in that strange place between this world and the next, I felt the cool marble tile against my cheek and watched the blood, is that my blood?, make interesting patterns as it seeped from my body. There was no pain, just a beautiful darkness and a ringing sound in my ears, but I did hope that no one had turned off my video taping system.

In spite of any psychic abilities I might have had, I didn't see this coming.

-Chapter 22-

Missing Miss Roxy

*T*he Palm Bay police quickly realized that they were not equipped to handle all of the evidence they had gathered from the Seaside Condominiums unit owned by Roxanne Porter. The worst crimes they typically encountered were an occasional burglary, bicycle theft, and domestic squabbles. There was some light weight drug trafficking for the tourists but nothing that amounted to serious felonies; lots of misdemeanor possession charges and intent to use.

The Brevard County sheriff took jurisdiction of the case of the missing woman when her vehicle was found in a strip mall parking lot just outside the Palm Bay city limits. The chief of police was only too happy to relinquish jurisdiction; let the county boys figure it out.

After reviewing the condo building's security tapes, the Sheriff, too, realized that he might be in over his head. There was a virtual parade of characters that didn't belong at Seaside Condominiums. He also watched an interesting video tape that had been found in the VCR, showing an office, location unknown, and a beautiful Asian woman working on some accounting ledger books. On the tape, the woman they now knew to be Roxanne Porter, currently missing, walked in and out of the tape. A second tape, found fallen behind the étagère holding the television and VCR equipment, was a bit more exciting and the Sheriff soon realized a crowd had gathered around him in the squad room.

The same Asian woman bookkeeper was engaged in a wide variety of sex acts, some with men and some with women. Someone commented that his tax accountant was fat and bald and he wondered where he could find a new one that looked like her.

One of the older deputies, a political junky and hard core Republican, recognized the woman.

"Holy shit, boss, that's Senator Whitmire's wife. I'd swear to it. They're from Georgia. She's also a big time Atlanta lawyer. I've seen her picture on television with him at fund raisers. His family is big into Paso Fino show horses too. Looks like she has or had a sideline, huh?"

The Sheriff turned off the VCR. "Okay, boys, that's enough for today. Get about your business." He took both tapes back into his office and locked them in a desk drawer, planning to have a more private review later. He felt the beginning stirrings of a hard on and couldn't deal with that with his men around.

What did all this mean? Where was Roxanne Porter and what was her connection to this beautiful hooker slash bookkeeper slash senator's wife?

After searching several law enforcement websites and making a few calls to men he knew were political insiders, he discovered that Roxanne Porter was the famous Buckhead Madam. He also learned that she was currently under investigation by the I.R.S. for possible tax fraud, tax evasion, and sex crimes. Now the woman was missing and presumed either dead or critically injured based on the amount of blood found in her apartment.

He called the Georgia Bureau of Investigations and told Agent Buck Satterfield what he had.

"Damn, Sheriff, looks like you done stepped into a hornet's nest with this one," Satterfield said, working his lips around a toothpick. "Where you reckon . . .wait, hold on a second."

Brevard County Sheriff Tommy Thompson was placed on hold and forced to listen to country western music, so he used the time to flip once more through his file on the missing woman. It looked to him like there had been many out of place characters going in and out of Seaside Condominiums on the night of her disappearance. Whether or not they were connected had yet to be established, but the two large black men

dressed in urban gangster clothing obviously didn't fit the typical Palm
Bay profile. Nor did the gorgeous black woman, whose face was hidden
by thick tresses of hair, large sunglasses, and a baseball cap and could not
be recognized.

"Sorry 'bout that," GBI agent Satterfield said, coming back on the line.
"I wanted to check out a bulletin that just came across my desk. Looks like
your missing woman has been found."

Even though she had not been paid, housekeeper Marta Santiago had
been working for *Hot'lanta Belles* for two years and felt an obligation to
Miss Roxy to come in to work and see what needed to be done.

The mansion seemed quiet and abandoned, but Marta used her key and
went in through the front door, calling out, "Hola? Anybody here?"

Her voice echoed through the empty foyer and parlor rooms, usually
filled with gaily dressed women and men in various stages of excitement.
No music seeped from the speakers and no one played the baby grand
piano that sat gathering dust in the mauve carpeted formal parlor to the
right of the foyer.

Marta closed the door and decided to go to Miss Roxy's office and see
if perhaps she was there or had left instructions on the chalk board she
used for staff assignments.

The only dead person Marta had ever seen was her poor mother, and
she had been lying in a mahogany coffin, beautifully dressed and smiling
much like she had done often in life. Finding her beloved employer, Miss
Roxy, quite dead on her office floor was surreal, horrible, and she screamed
at the sight.

"Ay, Dios mio," she screamed, starting to kneel down to touch her, then
deciding better of it and slowly backing out of the room.

Roxanne Porter's beautiful blonde hair was matted with dried blood,
and her white silk blouse and pants were mottled and stained with both
blood and other substances that Marta could not identify. She just knew
this was the worst thing she had ever seen.

She then ran from the room, frightened of the specter of death, and certainly not willing to touch the body to determine whether or not help could be rendered. Roxanne's blue eyes stared up at her coldly, holding none of the warmth that Marta had come to know.

From the front porch steps, she used her cell phone to call 9-1-1 and in garbled Spanglish, she told the operator to come quick.

Elle and Noir had raced back to Atlanta, anxious to get to the bottom of not only where Roxy had gone, but what her intentions were regarding them. Was she going to throw them to the I.R.S. like red meat to lions and take the heat off of herself? It was beginning to look that way.

Had Noir's thugs actually killed Roxy and lied about it? Were they just trying to get over on the two women? And Elle was still worried about the pieces of jade that she kept receiving and wondering if they were connected to the mess with Roxy.

They both knew that their first task, in spite of their heated attraction to each other, was to reconnect with their men and make them feel secure in their relationships. Both Noir and Elle knew that the basis of their current lifestyles was in large measure due to their men, even though both women were talented, beautiful, accomplished and strong. That was just the way of the world, as true today as it had been for generations. Behind strong women, there was often a weak man, sometimes trying to enter her, but always trying to control her; to own her. It was a price they were willing to pay - just part of the game of life - no more important or immoral than the sex for money they had engaged in at *Hot'lanta Belles*. Same game, just a different playing field with different rules.

Noir found Fabulous sound asleep on his side and slipped into bed next to him, curling herself around him. She began giving him soft sweet kisses against the back of his neck and tracing circles around his anus with her fingers. Soon she could feel him tensing up and beginning to respond and he rolled over on top of her.

"Welcome home, baby girl," he said kissing her deeply and rubbing himself against her.

Without warning, he slapped her hard across the face.

"Damn, Fab, what you do that for?" she asked, rubbing her face and beginning to cry.

"Just to let you know who in charge here, baby girl. Don't you be runnin' off and leavin' me no more." He kissed her reddened cheek and slid down to suckle at her breasts. "I don't give a fuck who momma be sick."

"Ooooh, do me, Fab," she cooed, "you know I love when you do that." She propped her head up on a pillow to watch his head moving hungrily from one breast to the other, wishing he was Elle. Her eyes were cold and wary, and her cheek still stung from his vicious blow. *That's gonna cost you, sucka,* she thought.

Elle had chosen to go to her office first, but called Harrison to let him know she was back in town.

"Oh, honey, I'm glad you're back. When are you coming home? I miss you," he said. "This big place just seems empty without you."

"Shortly, sweetheart. I just wanted to check for messages and drop off some tapes and paperwork from the depositions I took in Florida. I'll be home soon."

Depositions, she thought. *The only thing I took was Noir's tasty pussy. Guess I won't have any more of that for a while, more's the pity.*

She sighed and thumbed through her message slips, tossing most of them in the trash. None of this was going to matter worth a damn if she didn't find Roxy and make sure she didn't sell her out. *Roxy should just take her goddamn medicine like a grown woman,* she thought, *and leave everyone else out of it.* Confidentiality and protecting the privacy of others was the backbone of the sex business. When things get tough you aren't supposed to just cave in like a tunnel in the sand.

Where the hell is she, Elle wondered again.

Chapter 23

I fought the law and the law won

Thursday, 2:00 p.m.

Conference Room A at G.B.I. headquarters was crowded. At the request of the Atlanta Police Department, which held jurisdiction over the community of Buckhead, the G.B.I. was providing investigative, forensic and other support services. A plan was being prepared on how to logically coordinate information and proceed with crime scene analysis, manage the press, and specifically not to fuck up what everyone perceived to be a potential land mine laden public relations nightmare. Complicating matters was the federal level involvement of the F.B.I., primarily because they were filing charges against attorney Elle Corday-Whitmire for money laundering, racketeering, and crossing state lines for purposes of furthering those crimes, as well as conspiracy to murder.

The G.B.I. had a murder to solve and prosecute, and if you added in the prostitution business with possible political, government, and law enforcement collusion, well the shit was getting deeper by the minute.

When someone whose business was providing sex trade services primarily to men, well, when that person is brutally murdered and her 'little black book' is missing, the possibilities for the ruination of lives and careers were endless. The men gathered around the table had received clear marching orders: Get this thing buttoned up ASAP. Arrest someone, preferably someone from out of state and low profile, and get them under wraps.

There were to be no press leaks, no names, no perp walks down a phalanx of cameras, no tearful wives of politicians 'standing by their man' in front of phallic microphones. Obviously, there were powerful men in the tiled halls of public buildings all over Atlanta who were worried about their image, their reputations, their marriages, and perhaps their very freedom.

They had tried to avoid another possible mine field - animal rights activists - by giving the deceased Roxanne Porter's dog, Cooter, to Elle Corday-Whitmire, after calling Miz Porter's attorney and discovering that she had left a will naming Mrs. Corday-Whitmire as the dog's guardian.

The public information office of the G.B.I. knew that a murdered woman was news, but the sight of a small white dog with bloody paws would outrage television viewers like nothing else. Not even child abuse. The remainder of Miz Porter's will was basically irrelevant; the feds would likely confiscate the mansion, cars, jewelry, bank accounts, and anything else of value, based on the Rico Act and the money owed to the I.R.S. for her fraudulent tax returns. Her executor would handle the funeral and the paperwork once the body was released for burial.

There had been lots of evidence, forensic and otherwise, gathered from the mansion on Peachtree. Fingerprints were everywhere of course; the building housed large parties, staff members, and clients. The process had begun in an effort to identify them and the lead Atlanta P.D. detective, Dustin Hartley, firmly believed that some of his fellow law enforcement officers and probably many public officials would be linked by undeniable fingerprint evidence to the house of prostitution. You could call it an 'escort service' all you wanted to, but everyone knew it was a whore house, plain and simple.

That meant there were plenty of suspects to investigate - former employees, Stu Butler who was the in-house security expert, a former married lover, Dr. Poindexter, and Poindexter's wife who had threatened

Miz Porter in writing no less. Poindexter himself had been named in her will as a beneficiary, which made him of more interest as a murder suspect, but guilty of murder or not, he'd never see a dime from the estate.

Detective Hartley wasn't worried about himself - he was a homosexual in a long term relationship - so he figured, fuck it, let the chips fall where they may.

That attitude worried the very black, very prominent, and very Baptist mayor of Atlanta, whose wife was known to seek an open microphone with the zeal of a cat licking up warm cream. She loved the sound of her own voice, she adored the way she looked on camera with her beautiful, carefully chosen hats, and she especially loved being on the arm of Atlanta's mayor. She would mow down anyone who tried to get in her way, including the police or the general public, whom she held in supreme disdain.

The mood in the room altered minute by minute between serious police work, ass covering waffling, and sophomoric attempts at humor.

A serious approach was presented by the agent from the Financial Investigative Unit, who laid out for the group the charges that had been leveled against Roxanne Porter d/b/a *Hot'lanta Belles*, by the Internal Revenue Service. He charted a pattern for that business and three others, located in Nashville, Chicago, and Las Vegas, of phony bookkeeping, tax evasion, and illegal prostitution.

The ballistics expert stated that the shooter was probably at least six feet tall, based on the angle of the entry wound, but no gun had been found at the scene. They were going to extract the bullet at autopsy and see if a match could be made to any weapons in the database, but that was always a crap shoot. Without a gun to match it to, bullets were meaningless.

They discussed the implications of the federal Rico Act, which allows law enforcement to seize properties believed to have been acquired by illegal means. Meant originally as a way to go after drug smugglers, the Rico Act had in more recent years been expanded to incorporate terrorism, prostitution, murder for hire schemes, identity theft, and racketeering. The seizure of planes, boats, automobiles, homes, businesses, apartment buildings and jewelry had been a bonanza for law enforcement, from small town police departments to the hallowed halls of the F.B.I., with money following President Reagan's economic theory of trickle down economics.

Politicians and law enforcement officials in the broadly defined spider web of Atlanta proper were licking their chops over the possible confiscation of the beautiful Buckhead mansion, several expensive automobiles, some fur coats, and the phone numbers of some beautiful, exotic hookers who might just be willing to trade favors for a pass on arrest and prosecution.

The bounty was exciting; too bad they were getting access to it over the spilled blood of beautiful Roxanne Porter, whose body now lay in the coroner's morgue, awaiting autopsy.

"You could probably build a whole new woman from all the plastic and chemical enhancements in that woman's body," said one of the forensics investigators.

"Yeah, it would look a helluva lot like your blow up doll, Homer," answered one of the Atlanta P.D. officers who was there because he had been first on the scene of the murder.

By the end of the meeting it had been decided that the G.B.I. would take jurisdiction of state matters - they had the manpower and the expertise to analyze all the evidence - the F.B.I. would manage the federal aspects of the case.

Strings were being pulled, unseen by the men in Conference Room A, to ensure that certain names were kept out of the files, and thus out of the media. There had been three names of G.B.I. agents initially discovered from credit card receipts, and that was unacceptable to the powerful men in the state capitol. The Director of the G.B.I. is, after all, appointed by the Governor, so the daisy chain of evidence might just reach all the way to the top, or in this case, the bottom. Lives and careers could be ruined, shot in the heart just as surely as Roxanne Porter had been, and it would be wise to find her killer quickly, quietly, and allow the I.R.S. to proceed with its audit in a timely manner, just minus a few receipts here and there.

As the Director secretly watched the conference room on closed circuit video, he was amazed at how stupid men could be when it came to satisfying their carnal urges. Using a credit card to pay for a blow job seemed the height of stupidity, but he also knew that a man with a hard on is not thinking with the head on his shoulders. Pussy and the chasing after it had been the down fall of men since time began, and that, he knew, wasn't likely to change any time soon.

He also had a file folder on his desk marked Classified: Eyes Only. It had been messengered to him that morning from the Brevard County, Florida sheriff's office. In that file, a photo had been printed out from a security surveillance tape; a photo of a woman he knew very well to be Elle Corday-Whitmire, attorney at law, and wife of Senator Harrison T. Whitmire.

Director Keene had contributed heavily to Whitmire's opponent in the last senatorial election, because not only was he a life long Democrat, he despised the entire Whitmire family whom he believed to be elitist, white, rich Republicans. You see, Director Keene was the first black director of the G.B.I. and it was a 'come to Jesus' moment when he opened the file and realized that Elle Corday-Whitmire was obviously heavily involved in the disappearance and subsequent murder of the Buckhead Madam. She might have even worked for her. There were other images that had been captured on the security tape, but none of them mattered a whit to Director Keene. His heart was pounding with excitement at the prospect of jerking this woman to attention, like a dog at the end of a short leash. The only thing standing in his way was the F.B.I., who had her in custody.

So far, the agents around the conference table had determined that state charges could quickly be filed against her for conspiracy to murder, tampering with a crime scene, and prostitution. They couldn't put the gun in her hand or charge her directly with Roxanne Porter's murder, but that threshold might be reached soon, once all of the forensics and tapes from the Buckhead mansion had been thoroughly reviewed.

He pressed a button on his phone that connected him directly to the speaker phone in the conference room.

"Gentlemen, good afternoon."

The men exchanged 'what the fuck?' looks.

"Director," replied the Financial Investigations agent who recovered first, "good afternoon. We didn't realize you were monitoring the meeting, but we're honored."

"Cut the crap, Agent Doyle. Who's in charge of this cluster fuck?"

"Uh, that would be me, sir," answered Detective Dustin Hartley. "It's my case."

"Come see me then. Bring the file. Good day, gentlemen."

Thirty minutes later Detective Hartley left the G.B.I. building with his marching orders. The G.B.I. would finish up all the support work - forensics, autopsy results, ballistics - and there would be charges filed within forty-eight hours. Not the killer perhaps, but someone much more interesting to the press and Atlanta City Hall. That was what mattered. That and finding the madam's little black book. And if they could pin the murder on her, they'd do that too.

Chapter 24

Who's Your Daddy?

ita Moore was tired. A day of tennis with a ladies club luncheon sandwiched between matches, then a massage and manicure had left her feeling relaxed and yet restless. She knew she needed to slow down these days and concentrate on trying to mend fences with her daughter, who barely spoke to her, but that effort in itself was exhausting.

She felt that if she just kept moving, kept busy, her life would seem more fulfilled, more rewarding. Nothing, however, seemed to work. She felt empty, drained of life and hope. Where once she had been an optimistic do-gooder, these days she was more often morose and mysteriously sad about something she couldn't put her finger on.

After having enjoyed the experience of sponsoring Elle Corday during her Darlington School days, they had hosted two more girls, but then mysteriously they received no further assignments. Her calls to the school were not returned. When her thoughts turned to her husband Ted, she shut them off instantly, refusing to consider the unthinkable.

Her husband had been her best friend since junior high school; they had gone from buddies to lovers in the ninth grade and neither of them had ever slept with anyone else.

She had gone on to college but Ted was the son of a cabinet maker and had learned the trade early in life. He began working for his father right out of high school and had eventually established himself in the Rome community as 'the guy' to go to for custom cabinetry. His business, *Moore Cabinets For Less*, was now a multi-million dollar corporation with twelve locations throughout Georgia and eastern Alabama.

They lived well, had everything anyone could want, and yet Rita felt that she had somehow lost Ted. Not only lost him, but lost him to something she couldn't name. They still made love but it was perfunctory, almost ritualistic. It never varied. Same position, same number of thrusts (she had begun counting because she suspected as much), same words uttered each time. It never occurred to her to stray, however. She wanted only her husband and to keep him happy, but she had no idea how to go about it. He made her feel old and undesirable, but when she asked, he always assured her that she was the very epitome of beauty and sexiness. She had even bought hair dye and colored her pubic hair to cover the wiry gray strands she kept finding.

Friday was supposed to be the beginning of a lovely weekend. After her busy day of tennis and gossip with the girls over lunch, she and Ted had planned to get away for two days and she had reserved a two-bedroom cottage at lovely Callaway Gardens in Pine Mountain, and they were going to renew their wedding vows in a garden ceremony. Suzanne had promised to attend and to make sure she kept her promise, Rita had threatened her with loss of her generous allowance if she failed to show up.

Rita dropped her keys and tennis racket in the foyer and went straight to her dressing room to strip and shower. She called out to Ted, his truck was in the garage, but he didn't answer.

After a quick but refreshing shower, she checked herself in the mirror to make sure her pubic hair still looked dark and full. She was pleased to see that it did and believed that her visit from 'Miss Clairol' had taken twenty years off her age. She happily pulled on a robe and went in search of her husband.

She found him in his home office, sitting in his large leather desk chair, dead.

His head lolled to the side, and a gun was on the floor beside the chair.

"Oh, God, dear God, Ted," she screamed, falling to her knees with horror, dread, fear, and an unspeakable sadness that rolled over her like a wave at the beach.

When she could stand, she picked up the phone and dialed 9-1-1, telling them not to hurry, her husband was dead. But they should come anyway. Perhaps as some sort of defense mechanism, she began to make a mental list of things she needed to do.

Call Suzanne. Call Callaway Gardens and cancel so they wouldn't be charged as a no-show. Then, as quickly as the list making urge had come, it left, taking with it any bit of caring about anything. She was suddenly bereft of hope and felt desperately alone and helpless.

"What am I going to do, Ted? Why did you do this to me?"

She crawled over and put her head on his knee, and clung to him and weeping uncontrollably. She was still sobbing when the EMTs arrived, entering through the unlocked front door and calling to her through the house.

"In here," she called out, "down the hall to your right."

Following her voice, they found her, distraught and shaking her hands as if air-drying them, her usually well coifed blonde hair still wet from the shower and drying at odd angles. Her face was red and blotchy and one of the technicians gently led her into another room to check her blood pressure and give her a glass of water.

"Is there someone we could call for you, Miz Moore," he asked.

"No," she said. "There's no one."

"Well, you sit here and rest for a minute while we take care of Mr. Moore. That is Mr. Moore, right?"

"Yes, that's my husband, Ted. I guess he shot himself, right? That's what it looks like. Why would he do that? Why?"

"I don't have any idea, ma'am, but the sheriff will be here soon. He rolls out himself on a call like this. He may be able to tell you more than I can. You just relax until he gets here, okay?"

Soon she found herself alone in the house; the flashing lights, EMTs, police, everyone was gone. The coroner gave her his card and told her to call him about the autopsy and when she could claim the body for burial.

"It's pretty obvious this is a suicide, Ma'am, but by law we must perform an autopsy," he had explained. "We will be respectful of your husband's remains, don't you fret about that none."

His remains? Was this what their long marriage had come to?

She went into the kitchen, silent except for the hum of the ceiling fan, and fixed herself a glass of iced tea with a splash of bourbon in it.

Walking slowly, not sure what to expect, she tip-toed back down the hall and into Ted's study. Amazingly, there was no blood. *Someone must have cleaned it up*, she thought. *That was real nice.*

She knew there were probably things she should do. What were they? She called her daughter and ended up leaving her a voice mail. She began going through her husband's desk; something she would never have done if he were alive. She suddenly wanted to find out why he had done this. Why now? Had he left a note?

She found nothing but business related invoices, correspondence, and old golf score cards. There was a drawer with Father's Day, birthday and Christmas cards that he had saved. She noticed that the Father's Day cards had stopped when Suze was in the third grade. Strange. She tossed them back in the drawer and tried to open the bottom drawer, but it was locked. She rummaged around and found the key in another drawer, unlocked it, and found a navy blue bound scrap book; the old fashioned kind with rough construction paper pages that went out of style years ago.

Carrying the scrap book with her, she went back to the kitchen to freshen her drink, then got comfortable on the den sofa and opened the scrap book.

The first page contained a snap shot of Elle that she had never seen before, taken with a Polaroid camera. It must have been during Elle's first year in their home, as she looked not just young, but innocent and somehow stunningly vulnerable; more vulnerable than Rita Moore ever remembered Elle being. Elle was looking directly into the camera and smiling sweetly, leaning against the hood of Ted's pickup truck.

In magic marker, Ted had written 'my sweet baby doll' under the picture.

Rita turned the page, fearing what might come next. Her heart was pounding with a mixture of grief, shock and fear.

A newspaper article was taped to the next page; it told the story of the sad and untimely death of one of Elle's classmates. Fellow Darlington School basketball player, Sissy Allbritton, had apparently been killed in a hit and run accident. The police had no leads. There was another follow up article taped next to the first one on the one year anniversary of the girl's death, reiterating the case, and lamenting the fact that the police had never been able to solve the crime. Sissy's parents were devastated.

Once again, Ted had used a red marker to write 'good riddance to bad rubbish' at the bottom of the page.

"Ted, what the hell did you do?" Rita asked out loud.

She took a gulp of her bourbon laced tea and sat it down on the coffee table, for once not caring a damn about leaving a ring on the expensive hand-crafted burled wood.

The next two pages were filled with pictures of Elle, all of them taken while she was sleeping. Rita had never known that Elle slept nude, but obviously Ted did. He had captured Elle from every conceivable angle, using some kind of camera that allowed photos in a darkened room without using a flash that would certainly have awakened the girl. In two of the pictures, he had placed a baby doll next to her, and one of the pictures was a graphic close-up of Elle's crotch. In another, the lens had been completely filled by one young breast. The pictures all had a surreal quality to them, and Rita could only imagine her husband spending hours at night, when she was sleeping, creeping around the house with an expensive camera, invading poor Elle's privacy.

What else did you do, Ted? What in God's name did you do?

She needed another drink, but as she went to put the album down, an envelope fell to the floor, spilling snap shots like a deck of cards onto the carpet.

At first she didn't recognize the subject of the pictures. Then she realized that these pictures were older than those of Elle, taken with an older model Polaroid camera. They were all of another sleeping girl, her face never shown, but she too slept with a baby doll and no under panties.

The pictures showed small pre-pubescent breasts, and a childish, hairless crotch.

One picture clearly showed a birthmark on the girl's thigh, and Rita knew it was her daughter.

She couldn't breathe, and fell to the floor, gasping for air. Her ears were buzzing and her face felt hot, as though her head might explode from a severe blood pressure spike.

When she awoke, it was dark and she could hear the phone ringing, but sat up groggily and decided to ignore it. She had nothing to say to anyone. Her life was over, just as surely as Ted's was. He had killed them both. He had killed their whole family, and apparently others as well.

She stood and turned on a lamp, noticing that her drink had sweat, leaving a mess on the table's finish, but she didn't care. She stared at the hateful scrap book and noticed the stack of pictures of her child. She reached over and pulled them to her, then tore each one into tiny pieces, then went to the bathroom and flushed them down the toilet.

In spite of an inner resolve not to, she was drawn to the scrap book and the secrets that it must still hold. Should she look? She was torn, but knew that she ultimately must look at it, if for no other reason than to learn the full scope of her husband's sickening fall into madness. What else had he done?

She sat on the floor, her back propped against the sectional sofa where she and Ted had snuggled to watch movies and feed each other popcorn, and pulled the big book onto her lap.

Following the pictures of a sleeping Elle, was another newspaper clipping, now yellowing a bit, about the death of a college student named Kyle Jordan from Kansas, who had been mysteriously shot while on a turkey shoot with friends in Toccoa, Georgia. All of the other hunters had been questioned, their weapons checked as well, but no one was charged with the 'unfortunate incident'. Kyle's parents were devastated; they had spent every penny of their life savings to send him to college.

Rita remembered vaguely that Elle had dated a boy named Kyle for a while. Was this the same boy? Why would Ted have clipped this article if it had no connection to Elle. Then Rita also remembered the Thanksgiving that Ted had brought home a wild turkey, fresh caught, he had bragged, throwing the nasty thing in her kitchen sink and ordering her to clean and dress it. The proud hunter returning home with meat for the family.

She had thrown it in the trash can out back and cooked the one she had already bought and thawed out. So that was what he was doing; hunting a helluva lot more than turkey that year. He was killing rivals for Elle's affections. Or had this boy done something to Elle and Ted was punishing him? Either way, Kyle had paid the ultimate price for getting involved with her. Ted had scrawled 'hunting the hunter' in red marker.

The next four pages of the book were filled with more pictures of Elle, and in this series she was wide awake and posing for the camera. Although she wasn't smiling and certainly didn't look happy, she was obviously cooperating. She knew these were called 'money shots' by the magazines like Playboy and Hustler. Elle licked her own breast, Elle spread her legs wide, then used her fingers to fully open and display herself, and Elle presented her ass to the camera, spreading her cheeks as if inviting the camera (or the photographer) to come inside.

In spite of herself, Rita found herself becoming wet, throbbing, reacting to the graphic and sexual pictures. If they affected her that way, what had they done to poor Ted? He must have gone crazy over this girl, this wild child. Maybe this was all Elle's fault. After all, men can only stand so much and then they are going to fall head over pecker in love with what is offered to them.

Reluctantly, she turned the page and Elle's now fully developed body disappeared, replaced by more newspaper articles about her life, her law school graduation, her marriage to Senator Harrison T. Whitmire, and her career with Carlyle, Kilpatrick, and Powell in Atlanta. There was also a Wall Street Journal article about her 'magic touch' when it came to international mergers and acquisitions. Rita decided that the reporter must have gotten more than an interview with Elle to write such a glowing and atypical business article. She could practically see him drool. And Ted had followed it all from afar, apparently infatuated with her. He had used the marker to obliterate the faces of many men in the pictures, including the senator.

The next clipping was a newspaper article from only two days before, about the shooting death of the Buckhead Madam. Dateline Atlanta, the article told the story of the beautiful blonde woman's death at the hands of a mysterious shooter. The article mentioned that the madam, Roxanne Porter, had been under investigation for tax fraud and several other charges, and the reporter suggested that she was about to turn state's evidence and strike a plea bargain with prosecutors and the Internal Revenue Service. Before she could do that however, her attorney told the reporter that she had been gunned down in her own office by a 'cowardly low life' who had cut short the life of one of Atlanta's preeminent entrepreneurs, a provider of services to Atlanta's elite. Her escort business locations in three other cities were also being investigated, pending closure by local authorities in Las Vegas, Nashville, and Chicago.

"Lots of horny men in those cities for a while," Rita said out loud, scanning the article for any mention of suspects. She found none. Police had not solved the murder, but the reporter said inside sources had revealed that arrests were pending.

Ted had written 'sorry Roxy' next to the picture of the mansion, so Rita had no doubt who the shooter was.

The last page of the scrap book featured an 8x10 candid snap shot of Senator Whitmire, taken with a telephoto lens. The handsome senator was getting out of a limousine in front of a courthouse. Ted had written the words 'I vote for you next' in red magic marker across the edge of the photo.

"Oh, Ted, no wonder you felt so trapped. Look what that woman drove you to do."

She cried then, genuinely sobbed, pounding the book with her fists, sad and furious and hopeless at the overwhelming losses that had all come from the wake of this woman. Beautiful or not, she had no right to ruin lives and lure men into her web of adultery, deceit and debauchery.

At that very moment she began formulating a plan to get even with

Elle for taking away her husband and her life. Her burden became lighter as she shifted the load from her own shoulders to those of Elle, just as surely as by leaving the scrap book, Ted had shifted his burden to her.

Chapter 25

Bailing Out

E lle was shoved roughly into the bare-bones interview room to meet with her attorney, dressed now in a pair of khaki slacks and shirt two sizes too big for her. The designer dress, spike heels, black pearls, and jade necklace her mother had given her were gone, leaving her looking small and forlorn.

She brightened when Irving Loeb entered and sat across from her at the scarred Formica topped table.

He snapped open his briefcase, took out a notepad, and began questioning her.

"Elle, do you know what this is about?"

"Irv, I have no idea," she lied. "They arrested me at my reception like a common criminal. They won't even tell me what I'm charged with. I said I wasn't talking, wanted a lawyer, so they shoved me in a holding cell. They strip searched me for God's sake! What did they think I was hiding up my ass? A gun?"

"Well, I'm told the charges are related to the apparent murder of a Roxanne Porter, plus other federal charges including violations of the Rico Act, tax fraud, tax evasion, and money laundering. You need to be honest with me, Elle, if I'm going to help you."

"Roxanne Porter? She's dead? Oh, God, I was afraid of that. But I didn't kill her; I didn't have anything to do with that."

A horrified Loeb listened intently, taking notes, as Elle told him the entire story of her long relationship to Roxy, working her way through college and law school at *Hot'lanta Belles,* how she had helped Roxy keep her books, and how she and Noir had gone to Florida to look for her. She described finding the blood in Roxy's condo, and her fear that Roxy was being audited by the I.R.S. and was going to turn state's evidence and throw her to the feds for a plea deal.

She assured her lawyer that she was not guilty of any serious crime, only past prostitution, the proceeds of which she had never paid taxes on, and stated again that she had nothing to do with Roxy's death.

"If you need help verifying any of this, call Stu Butler. He knows Roxy and he knows me. He's a private investigator, an ex-cop, and he can give you lots of information about *Hot'lanta Belles.*"

The more Elle talked, the more convinced her attorney became that she was in deep trouble. As she explained her concern about Roxy throwing her to the wolves, a motive for murder became clear. He knew that was what the cops would think as well.

"Who else would want to kill her?" he asked.

"Who would want to kill a madam? The list is huge. How about disgruntled employees, cops who were afraid of being outed for their patronage of her facilities, and former girls like me who have moved on with their lives and don't want to be dragged down by her. I even saw a note once from Amelia Poindexter, her plastic surgeon boyfriend's wife, threatening to kill her. Plus, she was apparently taping everything that went on in the mansion! That's what I went to Florida to try to find. The tapes. I didn't want to kill her. I loved her actually, at least at one time I did."

"Elle, I can tell you this. I don't care how long the list of suspects is, I don't care if they have someone on tape shooting her and then giving a written confession, they're gonna go after you because of who you are. The politicians in this town will feast on your carcass like buzzards on road kill. So, I'm going to see if I can get you out on bail, but you need to seriously consider your options. This will be a long, dirty road. Do you have anything you can trade them?"

"I have her little black book," she said with a sly smile. "Maybe it has a few of their names it in. I also have a lot of the video tapes. Those might be of interest. Matter of fact, I'm sure I've seen one of the cops who arrested me in the mansion. Maybe there's a tape of him getting a blow job or begging for punishment from Dominatrix Juliana."

He stood up, tossed his notebook back in the briefcase, snapped it shut, and turned to leave.

"Those are some good bargaining chips, Elle. You should be out in forty-eight hours, if Harrison has to go to the damned President of the United States," he said. "As you might imagine, he's beside himself. He loves you very much. But I'm sure you know that."

"Yes, Irv, I know my husband loves me. Just make sure he gets me out. And for God's sake, don't tell him anything I've told you. He knows nothing about my past. I tried to tell him once and he shut me down, saying that his life began the day he met me, and he wanted to know nothing about anything before that day."

"Okay, no problem. We'll get you out of here then decide how to proceed with battling these charges. It's the federal charges I'm most concerned about. They probably can't prove you conspired to murder Roxanne Porter, I think they just threw that in for dramatic effect, to scare you into talking. Just keep your mouth shut is my advice."

"That I can do," she assured him. "That I can do."

Harrison was thrilled to see Irving Loeb coming out of the interrogation room, and rushed over to question him about Elle.

"Is she okay? How's she holding up?"

"She's smart, brave, and strong, Harrison. She'll be fine. She also has a few aces up her sleeve - aces the G.B.I. may not want to see the cold light of day."

"What aces? What are you talking about?" Harrison asked, suddenly hopeful.

"I can't discuss that with you - attorney client privilege you know. You just have to trust me to handle matters. Now let's you and me go see Judge Nevers and see if we can get her released on her own recognizance. He's a poker buddy of mine and presides in the federal district criminal courts. I think he'll play ball."

The two men pushed their way through an aggressive swarm of reporters, including both print and television, 'no commenting' until they reached Harrison's limousine and disappeared inside.

Irving Loeb scrolled through his cell phone contacts until he found the one he wanted.

"Hello, Pete. It's Irv. Got a minute?"

He laughed at the rude response he'd received, then got to the point, requesting an en camera emergency bond hearing at the earliest possible moment, which turned out to be ten o'clock the following morning.

"That'll have to do, Pete. Thanks. I'll let the F.B.I. attorney and any other alphabet agencies I can think of know to be there if they're interested. We can't leave this woman sitting in the goddamn lockup waiting on arraignment. Those arrogant federal fuckers will drag it out as long as they can and you know rich women, especially lawyers, don't do too well in jail."

He laughed again and disconnected, then called his assistant at home to let her know about informing all concerned parties to be in Federal Magistrate Peter Nevers' chambers by ten o'clock.

After a difficult night in jail, Elle was only too happy to find herself being driven in a panel van to her bail bond hearing. Even though the van was far from the limousine luxury she was accustomed to, and the windows were barred, she enjoyed the ride and tried to chat with the driver and guard. They didn't respond to her attempts at flirtation, however, and she used the majority of the hour spent barely moving in downtown Atlanta morning traffic to process the events of the last few days and how her life had begun spiraling out of control.

She had always maintained tight control on her life, making decisions, sometimes tough ones, based on how far she could move up the ladder. She wanted everything - power, unbridled sex, money, jewelry, love - all of it, in unlimited quantities. She had always been willing to do whatever it took to reach the pinnacle, and was nearly there, when it was snatched from her grasp. *Why?* She just couldn't quite put together the pieces of the puzzle. *Who killed Roxy*, she wondered. *And why am I being set up like this?*

No solutions came to her before the van jerked to a stop and she was pulled down the metal steps and shoved into the federal building, then placed in a cold gray holding room to await her fate. Even though she was an attorney, other than her law school days, she had not seen this side of the criminal courts system. She preferred the board rooms and wheeling and dealing in mergers and acquisitions, and still held out hope that some day she could get back to what she did best.

On a separate floor in the same building, Senator Whitmire, Elle's attorney Irving Loeb, and several attorneys representing the G.B.I., F.B.I. and I.R.S. gathered in Judge Nevers' paneled and austere chambers. Irving Loeb requested that his client, a member of the legal community in good standing with no criminal history, the wife of a United States senator, and innocent until proven guilty, be allowed her freedom.

His request for R.O.R. was rejected and a bail of one million dollars was set due to the seriousness of the charges, and the fact that additional charges were pending and likely to be filed within the week.

Harrison wrote a check and presented it to the court clerk with a flourish; he had considered bringing in cash but thought better of it, deciding it might look crass. He'd had to use his own money from his personal account, because his parents, especially his mother, were pressuring him to distance himself from Elle. He would never do that, but the entire Whitmire clan had gathered in itself, closing ranks, and pushing Elle to the outside. When she was slated to be a partner in a prominent Atlanta law firm, she was golden, but the minute she stepped in controversy and became associated in the news with criminal enterprises, prostitution, and, horror of horrors, murder, she was persona non grata. Harrison knew his mother, and knew that even if Elle were to be found innocent of all charges and completely exonerated, Mother Whitmire would never deign to be seen in her company again. It would just be too scandalous.

That was Harrison's frame of mind as he sat silently, allowing the attorney to make the arrangements. The only thing he was concerned with was getting Elle out of here and back in his arms. He couldn't wait to hold her, feel her soft curves against him, smell the incredible fragrance of her hair, and touch her warm skin. His 'little senator' began to stir and he moved around, focusing on the proceedings in process.

Soon the paper work was done and Elle was brought into the room, uncuffed, and released from custody. He folded her into his arms, determined to never let her go again. No matter what she had done, he loved her. She seemed so small and fragile, making him feel even more protective.

After thanking their attorney, who told them Elle's first court appearance would be in two weeks in the Federal Northern District of Georgia, with the infamous U.S. Attorney himself representing the people, and retrieving Elle's belongings from the bailiff, Harrison led her to his waiting limousine for the drive home.

He gave her one other bit of news; there had been a preliminary reading of Roxanne Porter's will and in a strange turn of events, she had left custody of her little dog, Cooter, to Elle. Someone would deliver the dog to Elle's home that afternoon.

Great, Elle thought. *That's just what I need. Something else to clean up after.*

Chapter 26

Screwed Again

Elle couldn't wait to get out of the horrid, ill-fitting jail uniform and take a long hot bubble bath with her favorite jasmine scented oils.

"Harrison, here," she said, tossing the shirt, pants and cotton underpanties to him. "Go put these in the fireplace and burn them. They stink!"

"Are you kidding?"

"No, I'm fucking serious, Harrison. I never want to see them or smell them again. Do it!"

There was a roughness to her voice, an edge that had not been there before, he realized, and he decided he better follow her instructions, even though he hated it when she used course language. He was always afraid that she would slip in front of his parents, who would be horrified at the 'f' word.

"Okay, but when I get back up here we need to talk."

"Sure, just take care of that for me, would you?" This time she softened her voice and smiled. "Thanks for getting me out of there, honey. I know how difficult that must have been. I could have been lost in the federal system for weeks without Irving pulling strings. We owe him a lot."

"I know," replied Harrison, leaving with the clothes bundled up in a khaki ball.

When he came back up stairs he found Elle sitting at her dressing table, combing her long wet hair, dressed only in a white Cosabella gown. She seemed to be looking at a row of stones lying on her dressing table.

"What are you looking at, babe?" he asked, standing behind her and placing his hands on her shoulders. He began kneading her neck and back, which he noticed felt tight and knotted.

"Nothing," she said, shifting her gaze to the mirror to meet his eyes in their reflection. "Oh, that feels incredibly good."

She leaned back and realized that he was becoming excited just from touching her. It felt good to know that she still had the power to affect him, even after his having seen her at her worst.

Power was her aphrodisiac, her pornography, her ultimate turn on. The look she saw in his eyes, the utter adoration he obviously felt, told her that he would do anything for her. Now that was power.

"Kiss the baby," she said, standing and turning toward him.

He lifted the gown by the hem, pulling it up and over her head, and tossing it to the floor. He then bent and softly kissed her **Pussy Power** tattoo, a ritual that had become a signature part of their love making. Before he could touch any other part of her, he had to pay homage to her power by kissing the symbol of that power. He didn't mind at all, because just below the tattoo his lips always traveled to her nipple, suckling from them, first one and then the other, which always seemed to please her.

This time she allowed him a few moments of gentle nuzzling, then pushed his head away.

"Harrison, stop. We need to talk for a moment. Then you may take me any way you wish tonight. I'm all yours." Her smile held the promise of untold sexual experiences.

"Sure, okay. But talk fast. I want you so badly I may spontaneously explode at any moment!"

"I take it your family is not thrilled with these developments? I would assume they want to distance themselves from their mixed breed slut of a daughter-in-law, right?"

"Oh, Elle, my heart, you know how they are. They'll come around in time. We're going to get you out of this mess and get our lives back on track. Let's don't spoil our night together worrying about them."

"I'm not worrying about them, I just want to get the lay of the land. Have you heard from my law firm? Have they rescinded my partnership offer?"

"Apparently they have. They messengered over a formal letter today, and I read it because I didn't know if it related to the charges or the hearing. It's on your desk downstairs. Screw them and the horse they road in on. Screw my family too. You can open your own law offices. The publicity will be good for you, you'll see." He smiled hopefully, but it was a weak smile and they both knew he was trying to put lipstick on a very ugly pig.

"So much for loyalty. Not that I expected them to stand by me, but they could have waited until the matter is adjudicated. They have 'innocent until *proven* guilty' stenciled in gold all over the offices. Hypocritical mother fuckers. You're right, fuck them."

Suddenly passionate, a passion fueled by anger and hurt, Elle pushed Harrison down on his back and straddled him.

"And speaking of fucking, my dear husband, I'm now going to fuck your loving, loyal as hell, brains out."

"Well, when you put it like that, the 'f' word sounds pretty damn good," Harrison said.

He pushed his palms against her erect nipples and closed his eyes, happy to lose himself in her aura of sensuality. On the senate floor he could wield power that affected the lives of millions, but between his wife's legs, he was a mere pawn, helpless and at her mercy.

She proceeded to ply all of the tricks of her old trade, everything she had learned in years of pleasing men, and each time Harrison approached climax, she would pull back just enough to hold him off and not allow release.

For two hours she alternated between using her tongue and fingers on him, and encouraging him to treat her body as a playground, even entering her anally, which was something she usually discouraged.

When she finally allowed him release and to explode inside her, he shuddered violently, like a ship hitting an iceberg, and fell onto his back, gasping for breath and glistening with sweat. As always, Elle found herself tired but strangely filled with a spiking energy. She was happy that he had been satisfied, he deserved it, but she was jittery and unsatisfied. There was a part of her that still yearned for satisfaction, and Harrison had never reached it. No matter how deeply he went inside her, whether with his long patrician fingers, his adequate penis or his tongue, he never reached her 'secret spot'.

They took a shower together, gently soaping and rubbing each other's bodies, lovingly enjoying the closeness and intimacy of the moment.

"Elle, do you know how much I love you?" he asked, when they were again in the bed, this time propped against a mountain of feather pillows.

"Mmmm hmmm," she murmured. "I know. I love you too."

"No, don't dismiss what I'm saying so easily. I want you to understand how much I love you. Saying those words doesn't come close to expressing how I feel. I would die for you, as easily as I would pour you a glass of wine, or enter your body. I want to crawl inside you and disappear. That's what I think about when we're making love. That's what I'm trying to do when I'm pushing myself up inside you. I'm trying to get all the way in, deep inside, and stay there."

She rolled over on her side to face him and said, "I do understand. And while I can't honestly say that my love approaches that level of frenzy, I do love you too. You are my solid rock that I can stand on in shifting sands. I will never leave you."

"It would kill me if you ever left me, Elle. Don't ever even say that again. Don't put those words out there for the fates to play with."

"Okay. But I won't, you know . . ." She smiled up at him teasingly.

"And there's one more thing I want to discuss. This whole incident has made me realize how much I want us to have a child. We need to create something permanent together, a legacy; a future. Will you go with me to see a doctor and see why we haven't conceived? Will you do that for me?"

"Of course, honey. If that will make you happy. As soon as this mess is over with, we'll go see a fertility specialist and get to the bottom of it. Pardon the pun." She smiled again, trying to lighten his mood.

"No, I don't want to wait until 'this mess' as you call it is cleared up. That could take months, or even years. You certainly know how the courts drag things out. Just knowing that we might have a child in our lives will give us the hope to get through this ordeal. I must have a piece of you, Elle. A tangible piece of you to hold. Something from your womb. Let's go this week. I'll make the appointment, okay?"

"Oh, Harrison, you are so wonderfully sweet and romantic," she replied, realizing that his fear was palpable, bordering on terror. "All right, if you insist we'll go, but I think you're being overly dramatic. Two people who can make love the way we do can't possibly have anything wrong with them. You probably just have some lazy, slow-ass Southern swimmers, that's all." *It's gotta be you,* she thought, *because I know I can conceive.*

She punched him playfully in the ribs and he finally laughed, thinking *It's gotta be you, my angel, because I got two girls pregnant in high school before I even had a driver's license.*

Exhaustion took over and they fell asleep in each other's arms. Harrison dreamed of standing over a baby's crib, looking down at a smiling infant. Elle dreamed of Noir; a dream that replayed their sexual escapades in the Florida motel room. She awoke to find her hand between her legs and Harrison snoring softly beside her.

Sometime during the night, Cooter had found his way into their room and was curled into a furry white ball at the foot of the bed, a reminder that the past is always as close as our shadow. The court administrator had delivered him to the house and turned him over to their housekeeper. She had walked and fed him, then left at the end of her shift, knowing that her master and mistress were having a reunion in their upstairs suite.

She knew better than to disturb them, and trusted that the little dog would find his way upstairs and not make any messes before they became aware of his presence. He was certainly cute, with fresh bows in his hair and one on his sculptured tail.

Finding him in her room, acting like he had always been there, Elle wondered again what Roxy's intentions had been. If she hated her enough to throw her to the F.B.I., why would she leave her the damn dog? Just one more question with no obvious answer.

-Chapter 27-

Successfully Screwed Again

The following morning, after Harrison had left for his office, promising to have his legislative intern call her with news of their doctor's appointment, Elle made a couple of phone calls herself, Cooter firmly planted at her feet.

First, she called her brother, Tommy, to see if he had seen the news coverage of her arrest. Of course, he had, but hadn't known what to do so he chose to do nothing. As usual, her family took the path of least resistance in all matters concerning Elle. After all, they figured, she had left them, believing herself to be too good for Pulaski, Virginia and her family.

Joo-Eun had passed away the year before, and although Elle had sent nearly a thousand dollars worth of flowers for the funeral service, she had not attended. She had been in the middle of a merger negotiation crisis, millions of dollars were at stake, and she simply couldn't afford to walk away. Her mother was gone; what good was attending her funeral going to do? It was the present and the future that mattered, not the past. She refused to derail her partnership track for a sentimental journey to Virginia.

"Do you ever think about our family, Elle?" her brother asked.

"Of course I do, Tommy. I worry about you and your wife and children, I wonder how you're doing, and if everyone is healthy. You know I send you money all the time to get things for the kids."

"No, that's not what I mean, Elle. I mean our heritage. We're not just

Americans. We have family in South Korea that we've never met. Do you ever wonder who they are, what kind of lives they lead? Do you ever think about any of that?"

"Can't say I do, Tommy. I try not to spend a lot of time worrying about the past. I prefer to concentrate on my American genes and my future. As far as I'm concerned, our mother left that country and came here for a reason. She was looking for a better life when she married our father, right? And she found it."

"I agree, but I still wonder if we're missing something by ignoring half of our genes. One of my kids, my middle daughter, looks so Korean, it's amazing. Genetics is a funny thing. One of these days, I'm gonna go there, if I can ever afford it. You've got money. You should go one day and look up our relatives. See if any of them remember our mother."

"Sure, Tommy. If I don't grow old and die in jail, I'll do that. I've gotta hang up now. Take care. Send me some pictures. Remember Auntie Elle to the kids and I'll send you another check soon. They could be freezing my bank accounts at any moment."

"Take care yourself, Elle. Don't worry, I'm sure things will work out okay for you. They always . . ." A fit of phlegmy coughing interrupted him, reminding her how he made his living. He sounded just like their father had. Disgusted and angry with his failure to realize that going under ground every day was killing him, she slammed down the phone. She knew that not only would he never visit his Korean relatives, he would probably never see his own grandchildren.

Thoroughly annoyed, she called Noir and arranged to meet her at the *Durty South Recordings* condominium. Visions of a furry white rug and a furry black pussy suddenly danced in her head like one of Fab's stylish hip hop videos.

Noir greeted Elle with a kiss on the cheek; they hadn't seen each other or even spoken since the night they had driven back to Atlanta from Palm Bay, all thoughts of their 'Thelma & Louise adventure' excitement erased by the sight of red-black blood coagulating in Roxy's bathroom.

"I guess you've seen all the fucking news," Elle said, dropping her purse into a four thousand dollar Eames chair that she didn't remember from her previous visit to the condo.

Realizing that some interior decorating had been done, she glanced anxiously around for the rug she had dreamed of, relieved to find it still spread out invitingly in front of the fireplace. The fireplace itself had been given a much more traditional mantel and surround, but what mattered was the rug. She had plans for that rug!

"I see you've made some decorating changes."

"Yeah, Fab hired that famous Tamie Mitchell and her interior design team 'cause he heard she travels around with the glitterati, doing stars' homes, shoppin' for them and all that Hollywood shit. You know him, girl he got to always have the best. She did a pretty good job don't you think?"

"Yes, it's absolutely beautiful. I'll have to call her next time I do any decorating. I'm just glad to see the rug is still here," she said, smiling at Noir.

"Yeah, Tamie wanted to get rid of it but I convinced her to keep it. There's more DNA on that rug than a CSI episode," she said, taking Elle by the hand and leading her toward the fireplace. "And yeah, I seen the news. You know they been questioning Stu Butler and old happy-needles Poindexter about Roxy's murder. Who do you think killed her ass?"

"They think I had something to do with it, but of course I didn't. I have no idea who killed her. And by the way, I haven't given them your name at all, Noir, so I'm hoping to keep you out of it. No point in getting you dragged into the mess, although as they go through Roxy's records they'll probably find out about you. That would be bad for Fab's business, although with hip hop, the murder of a white madam might just be considered a good thing. He could probably write a song about it. Isn't that what they do? Kill the 'hos?"

"You got that right, sugar, but thanks for keeping me out of it. I don't want nothin' to do with no federal investigation. I've fucked plenty of those limp dick G.B.I. and Atlanta P.D. assholes and if I have to, I'll trade that information if I ever do get picked up for questioning. I wouldn't give you a cup of warm piss for any of 'em."

She poured two glasses of chardonnay, handing one to Elle, and then taking a sip.

They both giggled as they realized the color of the wine was much like the cup of warm piss Noir had just alluded to.

"Noir, do you know what's going on with all of Roxy's property? I've been sort of out of the loop the last few days. What's the paper saying?"

"What I gather, the feds done took everything 'cept the house in Las Vegas. Turns out that was owned by a Nevada corporation Roxy set up. Pretty smart on her part. She musta figured that could be her getaway place if things ever got hot. Too bad she got herself burned before she could escape. Course, she shoulda thought of that before she decided to tape everybody and put people in jeopardy. That kinda shit's what gits folks killed."

"Very interesting. Yes, you're right. She should have stayed loyal to her people and not tried to save herself at the expense of others. That selfishness may have cost her her life. But enough of that. Noir, I'm hornier than a lonesome cowboy in a barn full of sheep. Or perhaps I should say, hornier than a pussy loving woman in a man's prison."

"Wow, you sure know how to sweet talk a girl," Noir said, "but I know just what you mean. I ain't had nothing but Fab's skinny pecker pokin' at me since we was in Florida. We had a good time down there in sunny old Florida, didn't we?"

"Yes, we did. You got any honey, honey?"

"I do, but something tells me we ain't gonna need it."

They simultaneously sat their empty wine glasses down on the fireplace mantel and fell into each other's arms, kissing, their tongues probing, searching deeply for some hidden inner satisfaction.

As they kissed, their hands roamed, tracing the now familiar contours of each other's bodies, chafing against the constraints of clothing, jewelry and undergarments.

Soon they were pulling at their clothing, ripping buttons and breaking zippers, until both women were naked, breasts erect with hardened excited nipples begging for the warmth of a mouth to suckle them. Once again, Noir was fascinated by the enigmatic tattoo above Elle's left breast, seeming to invite attention.

Now nothing stood between them and the warmth of skin on skin, mouth on skin, and fingers probing deeply into secret crevices that only they had dared explore.

Thousands of dollars worth of designer clothing lay strewn across the room, reduced to rags by the passionate forces of ecstasy, but neither of them cared.

The only thing Elle wore was her heirloom jade necklace, which she never took off. Frightened by the confiscation process during her arrest, she feared the separation. It was the one connection to her past and to her heritage that she cherished.

She stood, gazing out the window at the Atlanta skyline, as Noir sunk to her knees, her muscular tongue etching a soft wet trail down her body, until it reached her crotch. She began soft, tickling touches, the barest hint of a teasing lick, which combined with her warm breath soon had Elle bouncing on her toes and begging for more.

Noir continued to tease, licking at her furry labia, touching her clitoris, just barely, then moving away. As she teased Elle with her tongue, she rubbed her buttocks, first gently, then more forcefully, finally inserting her fingers into her anus and pushing gently downward. It was a powerful sensation that Elle had never experienced and she was amazed that after all this time, Noir could come up with something new. Her knees went weak.

Her vision glazed over and she could no longer see clearly. It was as though she had become a crotch; a vagina with arms and legs. Her world was centered now beneath Noir's tongue and she could barely breathe.

"Oh, God, Noir, eat me, goddamn it! Eat me out now or I'm going to go insane!"

She twisted her fingers in Noir's hair and pushed her backwards onto the white rug and suddenly her dream was coming, well, coming true. *Pardon the pun,* she thought.

She spun around, sitting on Noir's face, pumping up and down against her tongue, as she leaned down and began to taste the pleasures of Noir.

"Aaaahhhhh," she moaned, her mouth full of Noir, yet ready to explode in her own furious orgasm.

Once again Noir slipped her fingers into Elle's anus, and that pressure, that wonderful pressure, brought her to a climax of long pent up emotion. She shook and shivered as she came, drenching Noir's face, but Noir was now concentrating on her own pussy, as Elle began to seriously excite her with her tongue and fingers. She bit her clitoris and labia, little nipping bites, which created an unbelievable level of excitement, with that tinge of danger that begged the question 'how much can I stand'?

She reached around and grabbed a piece of discarded clothing, wiped her face, and rolled Elle over onto her back so that she could be on top. There was always a battle for control between the two strong women during their lovemaking. She kneeled over Elle's face, lowering and raising her pubis, teasing herself as she had done Elle. She wanted this to last, and by pushing down and then pulling away, pouring cold wine on herself then allowing Elle to lap it up, and exercising self control, before either of them could see well enough to know the time, a full hour had passed.

They both laughed when their pulses and temperatures lowered enough to allow them to stand and look around at the mess they had made.

"What am I going to wear home?" Elle wondered, as she examined her now buttonless two-hundred dollar silk blouse and gaping jeans zipper.

"Do not be concerned. I will provide you with something adequate from my closet," Noir replied, switching to her sophisticated persona and smiling devilishly. Walking naked into the next room she added, "I always keep extra clothing here for the occasions when Fab and I need to spend the night."

Soon they were both dressed again, wearing completely different outfits than the ones they had arrived in, and both hoping no one would notice. As Elle left, she assured Noir once again that she would do everything possible to keep her name out of the indictments and the press.

"I certainly hope you can do that, girl," Noir said, reverting to street. "*Hot'lanta Belles* is closed up tighter than a nun's ass and if something gits in the paper and Fab throws me out, I don't wanna go back to no out-call business, you know what I'm sayin'?"

"I do, Noir. I know what you're saying, in spite of the fact that your wonderful tongue speaks in two languages. Three if you count 'cunt' as a language. And I also know that I need you to stay free for afternoons like this."

She kissed her fingertips and touched them to Noir's crotch, waved goodbye, and walked out the door.

"I don't know when I'll see you again, Noir. I may go to jail, or Harrison may be able to pull some strings and cut me loose. Whatever happens, remember that I will keep you out of it as long as I can. Hang in there with your man and keep yourself safe. Not watching her back is what got Roxy killed."

Noir nodded, and felt the heat from Elle's touch long after she had left, a warmth that would turn out to be goodbye.

-Chapter 28-

Playing Doctor

arrison's intern had worked his Rolodex magic and arranged for an appointment for the couple with Atlanta's top fertility specialist, Dr. Richard Lowenstein of the renowned Atlanta Centre for Reproductive Medicine.

The center specialized in the latest of both diagnostic and treatment procedures, including in vitro fertilization, and was highly applauded for their informational seminars. The Whitmires felt they were indeed going to the best possible facility where answers and solutions would be forthcoming quickly.

Seated in black leather chairs with brass nail-head trim, Elle and Harrison held hands as they watched Dr. Lowenstein studying their case file.

Both had been thoroughly questioned and examined, and Harrison had provided a vile of ejaculate so that it could be evaluated for motility and sperm count. Both were confident that it was not their failing that was leading to the problem.

"Good morning, Mrs. Whitmire. Senator. You're here this morning to learn the results of our testing and medical history evaluations, right?"

"Yes, doctor," replied Harrison. "We are anxious to have a child and have not conceived on our own, in spite of the fact that we have never used birth control of any kind."

The doctor was envious of this man; he saw women's genitalia every day of his life, and sexual excitement had never been a problem for him, but during his examination of Elle he had become aroused, and it was happening again, just going over her file. He kept picturing his head between her legs, nothing between them except the thin latex of his gloves. He had even begun thinking about her, comparing other women's genitalia to hers during examinations. He knew it was wrong but he seemed powerless to stop the visions.

Elle noticed that the doctor had broken out into a sweat and his face was red.

"Doctor, are you all right?"

"Yes," he replied, pulling a Kleenex from the box on his credenza. "Just a bit warm in here, isn't it?"

Elle thought she knew what his problem was, but decided to play along. "Yes, I think so too." She let go of Harrison's hand and removed her suit jacket, revealing a thin white Pima cotton tee shirt under which she wore no bra. *Think about that, doctor feel good,* she thought.

"Well, let's get to it shall we?" he said, tearing his eyes away from her breasts and looking back down at the file folder. "It seems that, Senator Whitmire, you do have a slightly less than ideal sperm count, but the motility is excellent. The problem," he said, meeting Elle's eyes, "is with you, Mrs. Whitmire."

"What do you mean?" she asked, stunned by his accusatory tone. "What's wrong with me?"

"Apparently you were pregnant at one time, perhaps availing yourself of the services of an abortion clinic? I've seen this kind of thing before and it's almost a signature."

Harrison was stunned, and he stood up, ready to defend his wife.

"What the hell are you saying, doctor? How dare you accuse my wife of having an abortion? She's done no such thing!"

"Harrison, sit down," Elle said sternly. "There are things that you don't know about me. Things I have chosen not to tell you, and I won't tell them to you now, but I did have an abortion once, when I was in high school. I was raped and I had no choice but to end the pregnancy."

Harrison dropped back into his chair and looked at his wife, perplexed and confused. "Go on, dear. We need to talk about this. Who . . .?"

Turning back to the doctor and ignoring Harrison's question, Elle asked, "Doctor, what does the termination of that pregnancy have to do with my inability now to conceive? Did something happen that they didn't tell me?"

"You honestly don't know?" he asked, doubting her innocent act.

"The only thing I know is that they removed the thing that was growing within me. I recovered quickly and have never had a problem since then. Tell me what you know and stop playing games."

"Apparently, Mrs. Whitmire, the doctor, if he was a real doctor, who performed the procedure decided to render you childless. He surgically severed both of your fallopian tubes so that you cannot produce eggs. There's nothing there for your husband's sperm to fertilize. You will never have children. At least without some extraordinary methods being employed. As I said, I've seen this before from clinicians with an ax to grind against women, so to speak."

"And what would those extraordinary methods be?" Harrison asked, regaining his composure and suddenly determined to press forward.

"We could obtain the eggs from a donor, fertilize them with your sperm, Senator Whitmire, then implant them into Mrs. Whitmire's uterus. It would be expensive and sometimes takes years to produce results, but we've had some success."

"Well, we'll have to think about that, but I'm not inclined to have someone else's child," Elle replied. "Let's go, Harrison. We'll talk about this at home."

She stood and picked up her purse and jacket, bending just enough to give the doctor a view of her ample cleavage, which he would think about all afternoon, as he poked and prodded a variety of vaginas, none as beautiful as Elle's.

Seated in the rear of their chauffer driven limousine, Harrison turned to Elle.

"Honey, do you think you'd consider . . ."

"Shut up, Harrison. Don't even start talking to me about having some stranger's eggs implanted inside me. That's not going to happen. I can't have children, and that's that. It's not meant to be. You need to just get over that notion. Grow the hell up!"

For the second time that day, he was stunned. First to find out that she had been raped and then undergone an abortion when she was in high school, and now the cruelty in her voice. Grow up? This was his future she was dismissing so meanly. Then he was immediately overcome with remorse at even thinking such negative thoughts about her.

Look what she's been through, he thought. *She's been through hell and here I am adding to her burden. I do need to grow the hell up.*

"I'm so sorry, Elle. I didn't mean to pressure you. Especially with this trial coming up and your losing your partnership deal. This is just all too much to bear."

He lifted her hand and sweetly kissed it, touching his tongue to the soft palm, which he knew tickled and always made her laugh.

She didn't laugh, but she did smile at him, which brought the sun back into his life.

"It's all right, Harrison. We'll talk about this more after the trial. Perhaps adoption is an option. How would your parents like it if we adopted a Korean baby?"

"I don't care what they think, Elle. Whatever you decide you can live with, that's what we'll do, and to hell with them. Besides, I'm sure they'll love any child we introduce as their grandchild."

"We'll see."

He kissed her palm again and they rode silently to their next appointment, which was with Elle's attorney, Irving Loeb.

For the second time that day, the news was not good.

Loeb wasted no time with pleasantries and got right to the point, after serving the Whitmires coffee from simple white china mugs with the firm's logo discreetly imprinted around the rim.

"Things are not looking very positive for our side," he said, sitting behind his ornate black lacquered desk. "The prosecutors are playing hard ball."

"Have you offered them Roxy's little black book in exchange for a no jail time deal?" Elle asked. "And don't forget, I've got that huge container of tapes showing lots of powerful people getting fucked in a wide variety of ways."

Harrison had been made aware of Elle's past, but only in the broadest terms - she had worked as an escort to put herself through college and law school - but he had draped the knowledge with a haze of gauzy vagueness that allowed him to ignore it and believe his beautiful wife had been the victim of circumstances beyond her control.

Now he had learned that she had been raped. She'd had an abortion and not only didn't regret it, she was cold about it. Now these details of her 'work' were assaulting his carefully crafted images of Elle, and he didn't like it.

"If you two don't mind, I'm going to step out of the room for a few minutes," he said, kissing Elle on the cheek. "I'll be right outside if you need me, dear."

As soon as he had closed the door, Elle turned back to the lawyer. "Poor thing, I'm afraid I've shocked him today. But I can't pretend any more. He needs to grow up and face facts. He didn't marry Mary Poppins."

"No, that's true, Elle, but men do have their fantasies about their loved ones. We like to put you up on pedestals and men have been known to kill anyone attempting to pull you off."

"I know, Irv. I know." She took a deep breath to compose herself, then added, "So, are they unwilling to strike a plea bargain?"

"So far, I see no signs of willingness on the part of the F.B.I. The I.R.S. is still chewing over all of Roxy's books, and the G.B.I. is handling the investigation of her death, but the federal charges against you seem to be sticking. They are like sharks that smell blood in the water, and the idea of throwing the beautiful wife of a U.S. senator in the federal penitentiary is just too tasty for them to spit out. My experience tells me you might do as much as five years, but as harsh as that sounds, it would be in a Club Fed facility. They're really not too awful."

"Hmmm, well, I guess we'll see what happens in the hearing tomorrow," she said, suddenly feeling tired and sad. Not sad for herself, she could take whatever they could throw at her, but sad for Harrison. He loved her dearly and was probably going to pay a huge price for that love. Whether he deserved it or not.

Chapter 29

A Beautiful Day
for a Funeral

The day of my funeral dawned dreary and rainy, sort of typical for Atlanta this time of year, but I prefer to think that the world was sadder without me. It did come as a pleasant surprise to me, though, that my psychic sister in Cassadega was right, and I had the ability to attend my own funeral. I highly recommend it. If we could live our lives knowing what was going to happen after we're gone, we would probably all live a bit differently.

The carefully chosen Executor of my estate, my older brother Charles, had done a good job so far with carrying out my wishes and taking care of business once he was called and given the chance by the government. I was glad Cooter had been given to Elle. She might seem like a cold bitch to some, but I knew there was a warm heart beating beneath the tough as nails exterior. It might sound crude to some of you prissier folks, but I can tell you honestly that there's something about putting your face between someone's legs that lets you get a real sense of who they are. I highly recommend it. A much better truth detector than one of those electronic lie detectors the cops are so fond of these days.

I was also pleased to see that there was a good crowd, even though many of them were press, came to see the demise of the famous Buckhead Madam. All of my girls were there - not Elle or Noir of course - but the rest of them weren't too ashamed to show up. A few brave customers came; standing in the back, sunglasses on, probably hoping no one would speak to them. Even Garrett came and I was glad to see that he looked truly sad. He sent a beautiful, expensive spray of pink roses, my favorite, and was no doubt risking his wife's wrath just to be there.

There were a few cops there too, probably trying to see if my killer would show up. Of course, they had the taping system in my office if they really wanted the truth, but the truth was not their goal. Anything they did was just a show. They wanted to ruin Elle and God forbid the truth should get in their way. One of the video tape technicians 'accidentally' erased the portion of the tape clearly showing a man's hand holding the gun that shot me. I should have paid more attention to my psychic sister's words to beware of 'more'. I now know she meant 'Moore', another bit of perfect hind sight, right? But hey, he's joined me on this side of the cosmos now, and that's a good thing. I just wish Elle wasn't going to pay for something that crazy bastard did.

I don't know how Charles did it, but he managed to purchase a lovely plot in the old Piney Grove Cemetery on a hill near the Chattahoochee River. I have always loved history, and this land was purchased by the old church way back in 1826 and some of my plot-mates are slaves. It is not only beautiful here under the oak trees, quiet, secluded, and dignified, there is real poetic justice in spending the hereafter with people who were bought and sold just like me and my girls were. 'Course, we did it by choice and these poor souls didn't have a choice, but still, a pound of flesh is a pound of flesh and when you're sitting where I am, there ain't no color any more. One soul is the same color as another.

I chose my brother to carry out my wishes because I knew he would do a good job. He's always been the smartest of us six kids, and is honest to a fault. Once he found out how I made my living, he would never take a penny from me, so I knew he wouldn't steal my assets. Of course, now it was looking like the banks and the government would end up with pretty much everything, but that wasn't his fault.

He even found an old black minister to say a few kind words of prayer over me in a service that was short, but very beautiful I thought. He was an elegant old man with a jaunty red carnation on his lapel, and he spoke beautiful words about redemption and how the Lord loves all his children, even the sinners. It's been my experience that colored folks don't tend to be as judgmental as the whites, and are much more forgiving.

"We gather here today to say farewell to a beautiful child of God," he said, pointing toward the gold easel my brother had set up to display a large gilt framed portrait of me in a body-hugging silver sequined gown. Bless his heart, Charles had found that portrait hanging in an upstairs hallway at the mansion, and it's one of my favorite pictures of myself. Good instincts must run in the family.

"Saying goodbye is hard, yes it is, but it is also another way of saying 'I remember'. Remember the good times with Miz Porter. Remember the beautiful days. Do not allow grief to steal your memories. Do not allow tears to dilute the goodness in this child of God. Death is an important part of life's circle, designed by God to show his children that the life He has given us is most valuable. Without the finite ending that looms over us all, we would surely squander His gift of life with careless abandon."

Some of my girls cried and they all laid pink roses on the gorgeous solid bronze casket Charles paid over sixteen grand for. It was elegant and I was very happy that he had shown so much respect for his wayward sister. Listen, folks like to create stories about how hookers come from poor, destitute families where they didn't have a better option for their future. In my case, that just wasn't how it happened. I chose my path very deliberately. Right after high school, where I had been a cheerleader and president of the student council, I took a good look in the mirror and knew my best assets were my tits and ass. The first job I got was a topless dancer and I made more money than anybody I knew who was going to college. Then came lap dances, and my income grew, followed by full out sex for money. The first time I charged a man two hundred dollars for a backseat blow job, I knew I was on to something.

The goody-two-shoes girls I went to school with have never owned the kinds of cars, furs and jewelry I did. They never bought original paintings for cash money or made a man cry from the pure joy of a fantastic orgasm.

My line of work might not suit everyone, but I was born with all the right equipment for the job, and for me it was a match made in heaven.

Chapter 30

Uncle Sam Wants Elle

lle's day in federal district court dawned beautifully; clear blue skies and a warm breeze from the east. It was the kind of day she wished she was spending at *Cherokee Falls*, astride her favorite little Paso Fino mare, gliding effortlessly through the pecan orchard. Would she ever have another day like that, she wondered, as she took a seat at the defense table next to her attorney and two of his legal aids?

A phalanx of assistant U.S. attorneys and several I.R.S. agents crammed around the table across the aisle from Elle and her team, awaiting the entry of the judge.

"All rise," announced the bailiff. "Judge Hartman Ayers presiding in the Federal Northern District of the State of Georgia."

Everyone stood as the judge entered, wearing a flowing black robe, and seated himself grandly behind the raised bench. After arranging his papers and settling a pair of small gold spectacles on his long nose, he said, "You may all be seated. Are we ready to proceed?"

"The people are ready, Your Honor."

"The defense is ready, Your Honor."

"Elle Corday-Whitmire, how do you plead?"

"My client pleads not guilty to all charges, Your Honor," replied Loeb, placing an arm protectively around Elle. Four inches shorter than Elle, he had to raise his arm to do it.

"All right, Mr. Lewis," the judge said, addressing the prosecution, "you may begin."

By the time the judge announced the lunch break and that they would reconvene at two o'clock, Elle and her attorney were sure she was going to jail.

They had shown video tapes of Elle, apparently in the offices of *Hot'lanta Belles*, working diligently over a set of books. They had shown the security tape showing her arriving and leaving the Palm Bay condominium of the deceased Roxanne Porter. And, while they could not state that she was the shooter, they had shown the tape of Ms. Porter being shot.

During the lunch break, Loeb approached the lead assistant U.S. attorney once again about a plea deal.

"No jail time and she gives you the address book and the carton of tapes she has implicating several of the G.B.I.'s finest getting their rocks off," he said.

"Hey, fuck those guys," the attorney said. "We've got your client dead to rights and she's not walking. My boss and some of his buddies want blood, and that's what I'm giving them. Now go get your client a tourniquet because she's gonna need it, and let me eat my lunch."

Loeb went back to the table where Elle and Harrison were seated, sipping iced tea and picking over their food.

"No deal," he said sullenly. "They're out for blood, Elle. I'm afraid you might do some serious time. There's heavy pressure from way up the food chain, probably political." He looked at Harrison and added, "Your political opponents are trying to ruin you by ruining your wife. Sort of like screwing by proxy."

"So this is my fault?" Harrison asked, horrified at the thought.

"Of course it's not your fault," Elle said. "It's just one part of the puzzle." She turned to Loeb.

"Can you get us a continuance for a couple of days? Say I'm sick or something. I can even faint if you need me to."

"I'll see what I can do," he promised.

Once back in the courtroom, Elle laid her head down on the defense table and closed her eyes, feigning illness.

"Your Honor, may we request a short continuance? It seems that lunch did not sit well with my client. She needs to see a doctor," said Loeb, leaning solicitously over Elle and patting her gently on the back.

After consulting with his clerk, a very skeptical but by the book Judge Ayers, grudgingly granted a two day continuance.

"See that your client is fit as a fiddle, Mr. Loeb. The court frowns upon malingerers and frauds. Be ready to proceed without further delay. And bring a letter from her doctor for my clerk."

"Yes, Your Honor."

The gavel sounded sharply, ending the ordeal. At least for the moment.

Loeb went back to his office to prepare as best he could for his client's defense, and Harrison decided to go to his office and confer with his staff about the political implications of the trial and how it might affect his bid for re-election. He wanted to determine the level of fund raising that might be needed, as well as perhaps mending some fences or groveling to his family. Suddenly it all seemed overwhelming and he wished that he could just crawl into bed with his beautiful wife and sleep for a year.

What he found out was not good. Fund raising was nearly at a stand still, and his campaign manager had resigned. As a life-long friend of the senior Whitmire, Harrison's father, that was a shock that would have family implications as well. Harrison's primary donor was his father; he secretly funneled millions through back door and side door channels that were used for radio and television ads.

"Dad," he said, calling his father for the first time since the news had broken about Elle's arrest, "we need to talk."

"Nothing to talk about, son," he said, "long as you stay married to that woman. She's going to ruin you, and ruin our family too. You got to make a choice. Don't call me again until you tell me you're shed of her."

The connection was broken, and Harrison sat, holding the receiver in his hands, completely at a loss.

There would be no children. If his father had his way, there would be no Elle. And if things went as badly as Irving Loeb seemed to be painting them, there would be no senate seat.

What had seemed so bright and shining just a few weeks before had turned to a lump of coal in his hand. He dropped his head to his desk and wept.

Chapter 31

The Gift of the Magi

It was clear to Elle what she needed to do, and now that the judge had granted a short continuance, she would have time to put her plan into motion.

She called Stu and asked him to meet her at a small out of the way strip mall in Decatur. The run down mall had seen better days, and now held only a Vietnamese nail salon, a Mexican restaurant, and a liquor store. The rest of the businesses, including the anchor grocery store, had left for greener pastures.

When she arrived at the Las Cantinas café, Stu was drinking a Mexican beer and munching on warm tortilla chips, dipping them in the vile green salsa served up by a pregnant teenaged waitress.

"Iced tea," she ordered, "sweet."

"Si, dulce," the girl replied, waddling away.

"Well, sugar, long time no hear. What brings you back into my so called life?" Stu asked.

"Sorry, Stu, I know I've been inattentive, but it seems that my life has turned into a steaming pile of dog shit in a very short period of time."

"Seems so, darlin'. I've been readin' all about it in the paper. Sorry to hear about Roxy too. She was a good woman and didn't deserve what happened to her. She wouldn't have hurt a fly. I've been grilled four different times by the fuckers at the G.B.I. but there's not much I can tell 'em."

"Yes, too bad about Roxy. I wish I could have attended her funeral. I felt bad about not going. But, Stu, she was threatening people since she got audited by the I.R.S. That shit can get you killed, and it apparently did."

She sipped at the tea, which she found sickeningly sweet and too warm, then said, "But I need help. I need to leave the country and I can't fly commercial. Do you know anyone with a corporate or private jet?"

"Yep, I do. I did a lot of security work and some divorce surveillance for one of the Atlanta Braves. He's from Costa Rica and likes to be able to fly home anytime he pleases. Sonofabitch makes twenty million a year and only pitches clean up. Anyway, I could put a word in with him. When would you want to go? And where?"

"As soon as possible. Tomorrow even. As far as where, I'll tell the pilot and no one else. I'm going to disappear down a rat hole. Sorry, Stu, but it has to be that way. If you don't know where I am, you can't be held liable."

"Elle, that's some serious shit, skipping out on federal charges. You know that, right? You can't just come back from that. There will be federal warrants and they don't go away. I hope you know what you're doing."

"I know. I understand all that. But if I disappear maybe they'll leave Harrison alone, and his family will be thrilled that I'm gone. He will be devastated for a while, but he'll get over it and get on with his life. He deserves that. He doesn't deserve to be ruined by me and the bad decisions I've made. He just doesn't."

"All right, if you're sure, I'll set it up. I'll call you with the details. The jet may be busy, or out of service for maintenance. Who knows? He has it hangared at Charlie Brown Field. Do you know where that is? West of town?"

"Yeah, Fulton County Airport, I know where that is. Thank you, Stu. You're a life saver. How's your wife?"

"Let's not go there, okay, Elle? I don't want to discuss her with you. But understand this. You and me, we have a long history together, and I'd do anything for you, you know that. But after this, don't call me any more, okay? Just forget my number. I don't want any more of this blow back on me or my family. Prostitution is one thing, but this is serious federal shit. So you do your thing if you have to, but leave me the fuck out of it."

"Okay, Stu, I understand and I will honor your wishes. No need to be hateful. Believe it or not, I didn't bring any of this on myself. My life was ticking along like a Swiss watch and then Roxy started a grease fire that got out of control. People are still getting burned."

He stood up and threw a ten dollar bill down on the table. "I'll call you as soon as I know something, sugar. Take care and good luck to you. I hope you know what you're doing. And, one more thing. You missed a beautiful farewell to Roxy. Her funeral was nice. Even than shithead Poindexter showed up. You might have actually shed a tear."

Elle sat in the shoddy Mexican restaurant, stung by Stu's parting words. She sipped the warm iced tea, and wondered if she did indeed know what the hell she was doing.

Two hours later her cell phone chirped. She was in her dressing room throwing a few things into a carry on bag, and dropped it to answer the call.

"It's all set, darlin', but there's just one hitch."

"What's that, Stu?"

"You gotta get to the airport and leave this evening. The plane just came outa the service bay and is due to fly down to Costa Rica in three days to pick up the Lopez family and bring them to Atlanta for a play off game. It's now or never. The pilot's on dead time and he can use the extra cash."

"Fuck. Okay, I can do it. Tell him I'll be there in an hour. And thanks again, Stu. I love you, you know."

"I know. I love you too, but forget you ever heard my name. Now get going, and good luck."

She finished packing, called a taxi, and quickly wrote Harrison a note explaining that she was leaving the country for parts unknown. It was all for the best. She wished him happiness and urged him to find a wife who could bear him lots of children.

Grabbing the rest of her jewelry, including the mysterious jade stones and the notes that had accompanied them, she raced out the front door at the sound of the taxi's impatient horn, nearly colliding with the Federal Express delivery man.

"Elle Corday-Whitmire?" he asked.

"Yes," she replied, motioning to the taxi driver that she would be there in a moment.

"Sign here," he said, handing her an electronic receipt and tracking device, then thrusting a package at her.

She got her suitcase, laptop computer case, and the package safely stowed in the taxi, and gave the driver directions to Charlie Brown Field, the general aviation airport in Fulton County. She stared down at the FedEx package, wondering what in the world it was, and missed seeing the police car pull into her driveway.

It took just over a half hour to reach the airport and Elle was frantic, but the beautiful thirteen-passenger Embraer Legacy 600, engines whining, was pulled out onto the tarmac. A red carpet ran elegantly down the airstairs and onto the tarmac; the taxi slid to a stop and Elle stepped out onto the carpet.

She was impressed with the jet, which was painted a brilliant white with the Atlanta Braves' tomahawk insignia on the tail. The pilot and a crew member showed her onto the plane and she selected a seat on the dove gray mohair sofa. She placed her laptop computer bag and purse down next to her and laid the FedEx package on the marble coffee table, securely bolted to the floor in front of her.

"Where to today, Ma'am?" the pilot asked.

"Seoul, South Korea," she answered, smiling at his obvious shock.

"All right, but I need to file a flight plan and get some av charts in order. Make yourself comfortable. There's a fully stocked bar and some food in the aft compartment. We'll break ground as soon as I get a weather check, figure out a fuel stop, and receive clearance to take off."

He began to walk toward the cockpit, then turned and added, "This is going to be a long flight. Are you a member of the mile high club?"

"What's that?" she asked with mock innocence.

He gave her a finger wave over his shoulder, closed the air-stair door, secured the cabin for departure, and went to the cockpit. His crewmate settled into the right seat and they both donned headsets, then began going down their pre-flight check list and reading what Elle assumed were flight maps. They were filled with thousands of small numbers, lines and circles.

Once airborne, and after getting herself a Coke from the small refrigerator, Elle ripped open the FedEx package, noticing for the first time that the return address was the Moore's home in Rome, Georgia.

It seemed to be an old-fashioned scrap book, filled with photos and newspaper clippings.

She was quickly horrified by what the book revealed, and realized that it chronicled her past through the sick and twisted eyes of Ted Moore.

She thumbed through the pages of pictures, seeing the slow transformation of her own body through the camera's lens, remembering the first night she had watched Ted Moore rubbing the baby doll, then climbing into bed with her. Should she have screamed that night? Would things have turned out differently? Somehow she didn't think so. She would have still suffered the blame. She had always thought that if she quietly played along with him, gave him what he wanted, he would eventually tire of her and move on to something or someone else. Apparently he never had.

As she read his notes and the newspaper reports of Sissy's death, then Kyle's, and finally Roxy, she realized the extent of his madness. When she turned the page and saw Harrison's photo with the words 'I vote for you next', she also knew that her husband was in jeopardy. Ted Moore had slowly been killing everyone who had wronged her, at least through the hazy eyes of his insanity.

She was about to see if her cell phone would work, when she realized there was one more page.

She turned it, and Ted Moore's dead eyes stared out at her. There was a gaping bloody wound on the right side of his head and whoever took the picture had made certain that the camera captured the full extent of the horror.

The facing page held a hand-written note.

Elle,

I am sending this to you because it is your story. It is yours to own. We tried to offer you a place in our family and you chose to defile the love that we offered you.

You tempted, confused and lured my poor husband into something that he was not equipped to handle. You used your body to ruin him, to ruin our lives, and ultimately to kill him.

This is a picture of Ted. See what you did? You did this. I hope you are happy now. I see that you are a rich lawyer and you are married to a wealthy senator. My family is tortured and devastated because of you and the evil tricks you played on my poor husband. He was helpless to resist you.

I wish death upon you as surely as you have caused death to visit my home.

Rita Moore

Well, at least Harrison's safe, she thought, dropping her cell phone back onto the seat. *Ted Moore's crazy ass is dead, obviously from suicide.*

Elle decided to put the scrap book away for a while. She needed to digest all the implications and she had a terrible headache.

It suddenly occurred to her that it must have been Ted Moore sending her the pieces of jade, each time he eliminated one of her so called enemies on her behalf. The stones were trophies, or some kind of stone memory markers. Who knew what had gone on in his mind.

She rummaged through her suitcase until she found the zippered case into which she had thrown her jewelry, the jade stones, and the accompanying messages.

The first one, probably sent after he killed Sissy read:
Bad things happen to girls who don't play nice.

She tossed that aside and read the second one:

Bad things happen to boys
Who play with other men's toys.

She wished now that she had spent more time trying to figure out who was sending the notes and what they meant. Maybe she could have saved Roxy's life. What she could not figure out was how Ted Moore became involved with Roxy. Was he a customer? It didn't seem to make sense. She read the third note:

Jade is precious and must be taken care of at all cost.

The fourth stone had not been accompanied by a note, and had seemed to Elle when she received it, sitting ominously in a black velvet jewel box, that there was some kind of implied threat. A threat against whom?

Looks like it was either for himself, she thought, *or perhaps Harrison since he was going to be the next target.*

She swallowed three aspirin with the rest of the Coke, leaned her head back, and closed her eyes. What a fucking mess. At least Ted Moore was the one who was dead and he could not harm Harrison or anyone else ever again. She felt sorry for poor Rita, but knew that the woman had averted her eyes to her husband's sickness, not only with her but with their own daughter.

Harrison deserved to continue his political career without her nasty baggage, and she knew that there would be no shortage of women making a play for him.

There was a lot to do in the next few days. She had to send the scrapbook to her attorney so the police could close the murder book on Roxy and Ted's other victims. She should probably contact Noir and her brother and let them know where she was, vaguely, and see if perhaps Fabulous had any music industry contacts in the Far East. She was probably going to miss Noir the most. She would miss her unabashed honesty, her sexual energy, her body, and her incredible beauty. Would there be anyone like her in South Korea? Somehow she doubted it.

And once she got settled into a place to live in the capital, she would begin traveling throughout the southern provinces of South Korea, visiting the villages of Namwon and Gwangju that her mother had spoken about, and seeing what the Korean side of her gene pool looked like.

Perhaps on this journey she would be able to find peace among the Confucianistic ideals that somehow seemed to have survived even civil war in a modern democratic South Korea; peace that she had not been able to find in the ambition-driven United States.

Jade was an American. Who is Ellie Eun Mi Corday? Maybe beneath the hidden layers of atrocity within, she too would be found on this journey.

Epilogue

he housekeeper had forgotten her key and had to ring the bell.
There was no answer even though the mister's car was in the
driveway. She could hear the little dog barking inside the house.

She went around back to try the patio doors, which were frequently left
unlocked, and discovered that they were indeed not locked.

"Hello? Mister Whitmire? Anyone home?"

The dog raced past her and scampered through the open door, anxious
to do his business outside. What was wrong with him, she wondered. He
looked like he had gotten into a bottle of catsup.

"Come on, Cooter. Get back in here and let me clean you up before the
Missus sees you. She'll have a fit."

The dog refused to obey, so she shut the door, leaving him in the
yard.

"I'll get to you later, little man," she said, putting down her large purse
and calling out again for the home owners.

She began searching the house, going room to room, afraid that she
was going to catch someone naked or worse, the Whitmire's making love.
That had happened to her once already, and that was enough. She had not
been able to get that picture out of her mind for weeks.

The downstairs was clear, so she went up the stairs, calling out
repeatedly, but getting no response. She stood still and listened, but heard
nothing - not even the television or any of his favorite talk radio shows.
Usually when the mister was home, he kept Fox News on all the time,
listening for political news.

She peeked into every room in the upstairs, including the mister's office, and finally reached the master suite.

"Oh, Mister Whitmire," she said, finding Harrison sprawled out on the king sized bed. "I'm sorry to disturb you."

When he didn't answer, she stepped a bit closer, planning to remove his shoes and cover him up so that he could get a good nap.

Then she saw the blood.

The coroner ruled Harrison T. Whitmire's death a suicide, which was confirmed by the note he had left.

In the brief note, typed on his laptop computer, he simply stated that he could not live without his wife. There is only one letter difference between life and wife, he said, and her letter had made the difference.

Her note to him was crumpled on the floor beside the bed.

Also on the floor, lay an 8x10 glossy photo of a beautiful Korean-American boy, age two. On the back of the photo was the name and address of the international agency where the child had been placed awaiting adoption.